THE HEART SHALL CHOOSE

Roark is charming, but emotionally damaged by his broken marriage. Julia quit a relationship when she found her ex-boyfriend was exploiting her. Whilst Julia still hopes to find real love one day, Roark intends to shut love out of his life altogether. Working in a tour company together, their friendship grows — but can Julia storm the barriers that surround his heart? And can Roark forget the past and move on to a better future, before it's too late?

Books by Wendy Kremer
in the Linford Romance Library:

REAP THE WHIRLWIND
AT THE END OF THE RAINBOW
WHERE THE BLUEBELLS GROW WILD
WHEN WORDS GET IN THE WAY
COTTAGE IN THE COUNTRY
WAITING FOR A STAR TO FALL
SWINGS AND ROUNDABOUTS
KNAVE OF DIAMONDS
SPADES AND HEARTS
TAKING STEPS
I'LL BE WAITING
HEARTS AND CRAFTS

WENDY KREMER

THE HEART SHALL CHOOSE

Complete and Unabridged

LINFORD
Leicester

First published in Great Britain in 2011

First Linford Edition
published 2013

A catalogue record for this book is available
from the British Library.

ISBN 978–1–4448–1612–9

Published by
F. A. Thorpe (Publishing)
Anstey, Leicestershire

Set by Words & Graphics Ltd.
Anstey, Leicestershire
Printed and bound in Great Britain by
T. J. International Ltd., Padstow, Cornwall

This book is printed on acid-free paper

1

'So why do you want this job?' His eyes were dark, unblinking and demanding. His features were too thin and there was an air of remoteness about him. From the way he studied her, she also had the feeling he was used to being in command, and interviewing people. Julia admitted he was the kind of man who had an aura that attracted her, even though she didn't want to pay him any special attention.

She didn't hesitate. 'Because it sounds like an interesting job Mr Ellis, and because I need to earn more regular money than I'm doing at present.'

Sitting to his right a blonde beauty, with pale blue eyes and an aloof expression, lifted her pale eyebrows and gave him a knowing smile before she resumed her silent study of Julia.

Julia noted the exchange. She felt increasingly like a specimen under a magnifying glass.

Roark Ellis looked down and shuffled through the papers in front of him. He pulled out a sheet and began to summarise. 'You're single, you've a BA in history and German, you've worked in various hotels to help finance your studies and you live on the outskirts of London. Is that correct?' He scrutinised her quiet, oval face.

'Yes, that's correct.'

'What are you doing at present?'

'I'm still working in hotels, part-time, but I want to find something permanent, something that pays better wages.'

'You have a good degree, why haven't you found something a cut above waiting at tables in hotels.'

Lifting her chin and trying not to feel irritated, she replied, 'Someone has to wait at tables. Why not me? A degree may be a springboard, but you still need connections or extra qualifications if you want a permanent job somewhere. At the moment I don't have either.'

He held her glance. 'Surely you could manage a simple office job?'

She shrugged unconsciously. 'Office work is not my cup of tea. I enjoy being with people.'

He didn't comment.

His gaze was so direct it disconcerted her and she was glad when she noticed that the second man sitting opposite was giving her an encouraging smile. The two men resembled each other. They'd introduced themselves as Roark and Keith Ellis, so in all probability they were related.

Keith Ellis continued, sounding friendly. 'There's nothing wrong with not liking office work. Some of us love it, others don't.'

Julia found that the dour man, Roark Ellis, could smile and when he did it was an instantaneous improvement. He wasn't handsome in the classical sense, but there was definitely something captivating about those strong, masculine features.

'I didn't say there was, did I? I just wanted to point out that Miss Radford has a good degree and isn't utilising it properly, that's all.'

'Yes, you would find that hard to understand, wouldn't you?' The friendlier man with sympathetic brown eyes turned to Julia again. 'We need employees who enjoy being with people, so you obviously fit that criterion. We also need staff who are completely client-orientated and who work without complaint, and for as long as it's necessary for our guests to feel they're getting value for money. Do you think you could handle that?'

Julia nodded and concentrated her whole attention on Keith Ellis. She disregarded the other two, as much as she could. 'I'm used to treating customers with respect and courtesy no matter how difficult they are.'

He gave her a brief nod. 'What exactly have you been doing?'

She gave him a quiet smile. 'I've

waited at tables, helped in reception, decorated rooms for weddings and conferences, and even covered for a barman on a couple of occasions.'

The aloof man's dark eyebrows lifted and he asked, 'Which hotels?'

Julia fumbled in her shoulder bag, unfolded a sheet of paper, and pushed it across the shiny surface. 'I've listed them. Nearly all of them gave me a good reference. A few didn't, but probably only because the manager didn't know how to formulate a reference.' She coloured, and wished her brain worked slower than her mouth. Her remark wasn't clever; these people were management-level people and might think she was being disrespectful and nit-picking. 'If you'd like to see any, I'll be glad to forward them, of course. I thought it might seem overconfident to bring them along.'

She had large hazel eyes, dark brows and long lashes. Roark was glad they weren't blue; he would have been less inclined to study her face if they were.

5

He nodded absentmindedly. 'Send what you have to the personnel department.' With a hint of humour he continued, 'I can tell that you're a spontaneous character but that's not really an impediment because this job sometimes requires unconventional solutions, but our representatives have to be patient and well-mannered at all times even if chaos breaks out. You could cope with that?'

Julia coloured slightly, and nodded.

The blonde beauty butted in swiftly. 'Adverse remarks are out of place. You have to put the customer first at all times, whether they're right or wrong, and whether you like them or not.'

Julia looked straight at her. 'I assure you I can be the soul of discretion. The hotel guests and visitors were sometimes very demanding but I was always polite and respectful — no matter what.'

The woman looked sceptical and made another quick note on her pad.

The interview went on for a while

longer; asking how she'd react to imaginary situations, what her hobbies were, her ambitions.

Julia was not sorry when the serious man looked across at the other two and said, 'I think that's enough for the moment, agreed?'

The other two nodded.

'Thank you for coming Miss Radford. We'll be in touch when we've come to a decision, one way or the other.'

Julia got up and straightened her skirt. Her ash-blonde hair was cut neatly to follow the oval shape of her features; longer in the front than the back, and it swung gently over her cheeks as she pushed her chair back to its original position. She glanced at the three faces opposite, and her eyes skipped across Roark Ellis's face quickly. 'Thank you. Good morning.'

She turned and they watched her slim figure until she went through the door and closed it quietly behind her.

Roark Ellis's attention was still fixed

on the door. 'Hmm, not bad. She shows enterprise, she's intelligent, she's honest and she's attractive.'

Claudia Wellington glanced at her notes. She bit the top of her pen. 'She's too impulsive, and I wonder why she's not found a better job before now. After all, she finished her degree over one-and-a-half years ago.'

Roark tidied his papers. 'Good point that. We should have asked why. How many more on the list?'

Keith Ellis looked at a paper in front of him. 'Another four. I must say I was taken with her. She's a breath of fresh air; young, uncomplicated, and friendly. She's anxious to find a permanent job so she'll make an effort to do her best; that's good for us. Right, go ahead Claudia, fetch the next candidate please.'

On the train home, Julia thought about the interview, and hoped she hadn't made a complete hash of it. She'd seen the advert by chance in a glossy travel magazine. It was the first time in her life that she was glad she'd been for a dental check-up. She'd flipped through a travel magazine while she was in the waiting room and found the advert. With the permission of the dental receptionist, she'd ripped out the page, and applied.

She was fed up with badly paid part-time jobs. She decided it was about time to continue her training and get a postgraduate teacher's certificate. She'd been living with Gran for the last three months. Her problem was that postgraduate studies cost money, money she didn't have.

The sweet smell of a bowl of white carnations on the shiny sideboard filled the small living-room. Julia loved her gran to bits; she was seventy years old, on the plump side, with sharp blue eyes and thick curly grey hair.

Julia had spent more time with her grandmother recently than with her parents. Julia watched as Gran poured tea into china cups. A cup of tea, and a good think, was Gran's solution for all earthly problems. Julia mused that most of the time it did seem to work — for Gran, but not always for her. Mrs Radford handed her granddaughter a cup.

'Well, at least they didn't just say, 'thank you for coming' and dismiss you. That's a good sign. What were the people like?'

Julia took a sip. 'Okay. There were two men and one woman. The woman was a bit toffee-nosed, you know the type, all chignon and pearls. I think the two men were brothers, or at least related. One was stand-offish but the other was much friendlier.'

'And you liked the sound of the job?'

'Yes, it sounds interesting and glamorous, although it probably isn't. Hostess's jobs never are, but Likely Prospects is a renowned travel company, and very exclusive. I could have two good holidays for the cost of one of their tours.'

'They didn't say where the successful applicant would be working?'

'I didn't want to ask. I thought it might sound brash. They specialise in tours all over the place — Europe, America, and the Middle East. My German is good but my French is less than average. They couldn't put me in charge of a tour in a French-speaking country — not with much confidence.'

Her gran tut-tutted. 'They wouldn't have interviewed you if that was so important. Think how many languages there are in Europe; they can't afford to have a travel representative for every language. English is the second language in most countries these days.'

Julia wrinkled her nose and smiled. 'You're right, of course. I think my working experience in hotels stood me in good stead.'

Gran nodded. 'It doesn't sound like it went off too badly. Don't worry about it any more. It's over and done with now.'

'I'd be thrilled to bits if I get the job! I could save almost all my wages towards the postgraduate course; the cost of my food and lodgings comes with the job. A couple of months with them would be enough. I hate being a burden to you.'

Mrs Radford got up and took her granddaughter into her arms for a quick hug. 'You are not a burden. You never were, and you never will be. I'm mad that Mike treated you like that, and I always will be, but I'm sure that something good is round the corner for you. If it's not this job, then it'll be something else. And I love having you here with me, so no more foolish talk about being a burden.'

Julia's eyes misted over and her gran looked down at her wristwatch to conceal her own emotions. 'Oh, heavens! I must hurry, or I'll miss my game of bridge. I hope to be back in time for *Strictly Come Dancing*. Are you working this evening?'

Julia shook her head. 'They'll phone when they need me again. I'll record *Strictly* if you like, so don't panic. Off you go. What's for supper?'

'Welsh rarebit. I got a lovely piece of cheese off Fred this morning. I talked him into letting me have it fifty pence cheaper because the edge of it was crumbling away.'

Julia chuckled. 'I'll make it for us both when you come home.'

A few minutes later, Julia watched her gran rushing down the small front garden path tightening her scarf and with her coat flying in the wind. There was a trace of her perfume mingling with the scent of the carnations. Right now, Gran was leading a more colourful and busy life than her twenty-five-year-old granddaughter!

★   ★   ★

Julia heard the letters falling on the carpet with a thud. She skipped down the narrow stairs and picked them up. Flipping through them her breath caught in her throat and her pulse intensified when she saw the Likely Prospects logo. She deposited the others on the stairs beside her and slit the envelope with her finger. Her eyes skimmed the lines, and then she whooped and did a tribal dance down the remaining steps. Gran came out of the kitchen, half-eaten toast in hand, to see what was going on.

Julia grabbed her and gave her a hug. 'I've got it! They've offered me a six-month contract, with a six-month extension if we are both happy with the situation after that.' Her face was split in two with a wide smile.

'Oh, that's wonderful. When do you start? Where will you be going? Come into the kitchen and have some breakfast. We've one of those miniature bottles of sparkling wine from Aldi in the fridge. We'll celebrate!'

Feeling on cloud nine, Julia followed her and read the letter again. 'I'll hear more details when I meet this woman. Apparently, she's called Claudia Wellington and she's department head in the company. She mentions she was at the interview so it must be that blonde woman I told you about.' Julia leaned back in the wooden kitchen chair. 'I didn't like her much but perhaps I won't have very much to do with her. I need this job and I'm determined to make a success of it and earn all that lovely money. Pour me a big glass of that bubbly, Gran!'

*   *   *

Julia sat straight-backed opposite Claudia Wellington in Claudia's office. Claudia looked down at a sheet of paper. 'Well, Miss Radford. Briefly, you'll start off by accompanying one of our other tour assistants on a weekend tour to Paris, so that she can show you the ropes and you can see what's expected of you. Three days later, you take charge of an eight-day tour of the border area between France and Germany. Mrs Lucinda Yeats is the accompanying lecturer. She studied French literature at Cambridge and now lives in the area. Here are the two itineraries. You'll see that we arrange everything down to the last detail, but if any problems crop up, our travel assistants are the on-the-spot trouble-shooters. Naturally, you always check back with this office at the first possible opportunity if you need to change any arrangements drastically. From the start of the tour until you return, you act as a glorified nanny to the group.' Claudia glanced up, her expression was bland and non-committal. Her blue eyes weren't exactly unfriendly, but they weren't welcoming either.

Julia nodded and waited.

'You always pick up any travel documentation here a day beforehand, and it will include the usual instructions and emergency numbers.'

Claudia handed her the itineraries and another glossy brochure with perfectly manicured painted fingers. She eyed Julia's trouser suit. 'We expect our representatives to wear our uniform at all times; a simple navy skirt and a red jacket. You'll be issued with three skirts, two jackets, a hat, a couple of red and blue silk scarves, and some white easy-care blouses. Go down to Mrs Walters in room 207, she'll sort you out. Wear the jacket at all times, unless it's unbearably hot. There's a short description of how to handle a tour, greeting the group, making sure people rotate the seating arrangements in a bus, checking in and out etc. Read it through carefully. Presents of money are not to be accepted under any circumstances. Accepting tips is forbidden, you're paid to do a job and if anyone offers a tip or a present, politely refuse.'

If Claudia expected Júlia to be disconcerted about wearing a uniform, she'd be disappointed. Julia was glad that she wouldn't face the problem of what to wear all the time. She relaxed slightly.

'If you have any more questions, don't hesitate to get in touch.' She got up. 'This is a friendly company, so please call me Claudia.'

Julia gave her a tentative smile. 'Thanks, Claudia.'

On the train home with her uniform in a big bag, she studied the itinerary and the brochure. The itineraries were straightforward, and if she wasn't kept too busy she might be able to join in some of the sightseeing now and then.

The brochure was about the company, their aims, and the correct handling of guests. The picture on the front cover was of the Chief Executive Keith Ellis, the friendlier of the two men at her interview. There was no reference to Roark Ellis, although various other company employees were listed and pictured.

Organisation seemed to be the keyword. All travel arrangements were fixed and arranged, and there were even suggestions for evening entertainment when tour members wanted to explore on their own. Tour attendants were expected to be available at all times. Julia leaned back and watched the passing scenery whizzing by; it sounded like a challenge, but if the itineraries were as good as they looked, the tours might be just as enjoyable for her as for the guests. She was flexible, she was friendly, and she was curious. She was going to do this job properly.

2

The trip to Paris gave her an insight into how things were organised, and she even managed to have some moments to enjoy Paris on her own.

Her first solo tour went well even though Julia discovered that every group had someone who always complained, someone who always came late, and someone who was likeable from the first minute to the last. The accompanying lecturer was a nice woman and they got on well.

Her second tour started at St Goarshausen, travelled leisurely along the Rhine by bus to Rüdesheim, and visited castles and other points of interest along the way. The group was full of enthusiasm for the fabulous scenery, their lecturer, and the good food and accommodation.

After saying goodbye to them, Julia went direct to the company offices. On her way to Claudia's office with her paperwork, she met Keith Ellis in the corridor. He had his arms full of colourful folders but came to a halt when he saw her approaching.

'Hello Julia!' He studied her closely. 'I must say the uniform suits you. It's very chic!'

Julia's hazel eyes twinkled. 'Thank you.'

He smiled and Keith admired the neatly cut hair that clung to the shape of her head and how the classical lines of the pencil skirt and shaped jacket emphasised her slim, attractive figure. 'How did it go?'

'Good — as far as I can tell. Perhaps you'll get complaints about something once they get home.'

He laughed softly. 'If there'd been any whinging we'd have heard by now. People are slow to praise, and very swift to complain. Where is your next tour going?'

'I'm on my way to Claudia, to give her the paperwork from this one and to find out.'

He rubbed the side of his nose with his finger. 'If I remember rightly, I think it's Basilicata.'

'Basilicata? I know that I'm showing my ignorance to my boss, but where's that?'

He smiled. 'Roughly between the heel and the toe at the bottom of Italy; it's not a very well-known tourist area yet, but a very interesting region and full of history. Roark will be the lecturer on the tour.'

Julia nodded, her interest growing.

'Roark's my brother. He read archaeology at Cambridge, and he specialises in the Middle Age and Renaissance periods. Now and then he takes on a tour, if it fits in with his other commitments.'

'Oh, I see. And he's particularly interested in this area of Italy?'

'Yes, so it seems. He knows it very well.'

Julia hesitated but decided to go ahead anyway. 'Your brother is a full-time lecturer for Likely Prospects?'

He smiled, but shook his head. 'He's a full-time lecturer, but he only helps us out when he can. He's helped ever since I founded the company, and I still drag him in when I'm interviewing people. I've found he's far better at assessing people's abilities and weaknesses than I am.'

Julia nodded. Someone opened a door further down the corridor and Keith smiled. 'Well, good luck. I'd better get on.'

'Yes; thanks Mr Ellis . . . and thank you for giving me a chance.'

Keith liked her and her friendly, open personality. 'You were well qualified, and I don't think we made a bad choice. Do a good job, that's thanks enough!'

He went on his way and Julia headed in the opposite direction.

*   *   *

Claudia was positioned behind her desk, as poised and well-groomed as ever. Julia handed her the documents from her finished tour.

'There's nothing unusual to report, Claudia. Mrs Flesch did a very good job and the organisation was perfect. There were some people who couldn't walk far but we usually left them somewhere close to the bus route and picked them up later. They seemed happy to drink coffee and watch the world go by. They didn't complain then, or later.'

Claudia fussed with the papers. 'It's always the same. We warn people in advance if there's walking involved, and how much. I don't know if they don't take notice, or if they deliberately misjudge their own abilities.'

Julia shrugged. 'These people didn't seem to mind.'

A shadow of annoyance still clung to Claudia's face when she said, 'You have three days off, and then the next tour goes to Basilicata; here are the details.'

She handed Julia a folder.

'Mr Ellis just told me I might be going there. I've never heard of it.'

Claudia lifted her pale eyebrows. 'It's important to have sound geographical knowledge in this job. Perhaps you ought to study some maps of Europe.'

'Oh, I'll find out all about Basilicata now I know I'm going there. I'll call at the library on the way home and borrow some books.'

Claudia looked down at the desk and patted her tidy hair into place again. 'Actually, I'm thinking of coming myself. There are a couple of picnic lunches to be organised and a travel assistant can't be in two places at once.'

Julia's heart plummeted. First, there was the serious Roark Ellis as lecturer, and now Miss Perfect was planning to come along too.

She kept her expression bland. Generally, she got on with most people, but she sensed from the start that she and Claudia were on different wavelengths. If Claudia came, Claudia would be in charge, and Julia would be reduced to a general dog's body.

Julia consoled herself with the reflection that she was here to save money and she'd put up with a great deal to reach her goal. Confused, though, she remarked, 'Why can't a picnic lunch be organised from here in advance like everything else is?'

'Because it can't, that's why! You can't rely on local people coming up to scratch. Hotels and tourist centres are generally okay, but if you involve the locals out in the wilderness, you're heading for trouble. In the past, they've often decided to have a siesta, failed to remember the order, or delivered too late. Someone needs to sit on their tails and ensure they understand what we want, and provide what they promise on time. Our company has very high standards.'

The prospects were getting better by the minute.

Julia guessed that the picnic table would be her responsibility. She was still new to the job, couldn't speak a word of Italian, and didn't know a thing about the region of Basilicata. In addition to that, the accompanying lecturer probably disapproved of her, and Claudia would be on the spot to dole out the pepper as soon as the slightest thing went wrong. It didn't sound like it was going to be a dream tour.

* * *

For once, the late English summer produced some perfect weather. Julia's few days at home were long and relaxing. Today, the final one, the sky was cloudless, the temperatures were mild, and the sun sent its golden rays all over the garden, bathing it in shades of yellow and jonquil.

She was slumped in one of Gran's old-fashioned deckchairs; the coloured stripes had faded, but the frames were still sound and it was perfect for lounging.

Between bouts of reading about Basilicata, Julia had weeded Gran's small flowerbed along the fence and listened to Gran's small talk about the church bazaar while sharing a cup of tea. Luxury hotels were fine, but being here with Gran was better.

She now knew that Basilicata was a region of verdant and rolling hills, that it was famous for the Sassi — hundreds of caves that had been inhabited for over a thousand years in the town of Matera, and that the area had numerous fortresses, Romanesque churches and Ancient Greek settlements.

It sounded very interesting, and despite her misgivings about her travelling companions, Julia was looking forward to it.

⋆   ⋆   ⋆

The flight left Gatwick at lunchtime. One of the guests rushed in at the last minute, but now they were all settled in the plane and making the first tentative conversations among themselves.

Julia sat at the back of the group and noted that Claudia was sitting next to Roark Ellis at the front. She'd spoken with Claudia on her arrival, just the usual kind of greetings, and then Claudia handed her the folder with the itinerary and pointed her in the direction of the early arrivals to introduce herself, and make them welcome. Julia noticed that even though Claudia was wearing a navy skirt and a white blouse, both were not company issue — the skirt didn't show the slightest wrinkle and the blouse was heavy silk. Roark Ellis arrived well before time and managed to give her a brief nod.

On arrival in Bari, a coach was waiting to take them to Matera where the tour was based for the two weeks.

There were nineteen guests. When the luggage was stored in the coach and people settled, Julia heard some murmurs of dissatisfaction because Claudia announced the front seat next to the driver would be occupied by herself and the tour lecturer, without mentioning for how long. It was generally company policy to 'rotate' seats every day, so that everyone had a chance to sit in the popular or less popular places. The travel assistants organised it and it worked well because everyone was halfway satisfied with the results.

Julia wondered if Claudia would give way, once the tour was underway; somehow, she didn't think so. Claudia had been with the company much longer, so Julia didn't intend to argue with her, unless one of the tour participants complained to her.

The road bent and zigzagged through attractive countryside; it passed quaint-looking Italian villages, old churches, fortresses and various other points of interest. They passed something that looked like the Arch of Constantine in Rome; it was much smaller, but very similar.

An hour later, they approached Matera and the road wound upwards through the town towards the silhouette of a cathedral. The houses were huddled together and Julia was fascinated to see the Sassi; houses attractively tiered out of the rock along the two ravines that lunged into the heart of the town. They had been lived in for over a thousand years and only recently saved from degenerating into a slum area. They were now coveted places of residence again.

Their hotel had been created out of some of these caves and she and Claudia handed out room keys in a domed, stonework foyer that was cool and full of atmosphere. Gradually the foyer emptied and the noise faded. The rest of the afternoon was free for everyone to adjust and relax. After a special welcoming drink and dinner, this evening was also free for tour members to enjoy as they wished.

Claudia checked the list once again. 'That's it! Let's hope we don't get too much quibbling from the guests. The hotel only has thirty rooms and there isn't much leeway.'

Julia looked around, smiling. 'It's lovely, isn't it? A completely different kind of hotel.'

Claudia jingled a set of keys in her hand. 'We tried the Hilton last time, but admittedly this place is more impressive and quite unique. Roark likes it here because it's in the old part of the town.' She moved off towards the stairs. 'We're sharing a room. I'll go ahead and check. Will you ask the reception for street plans? Perhaps they can provide us with a bundle, or make photocopies of what they have. We need at least twenty. Most people will use the time to have a shower now and take a siesta — me included.' She rounded the corner and disappeared from view.

Julia didn't look forward to the prospect of sharing a room with Claudia, but perhaps it would help smooth things over between them. She only hoped there'd be enough water left for her to have a shower when Claudia was finished. She made her way to the reception desk and was glad the girl spoke such good English.

Claudia had chosen the bed nearest the window. She was lying there with her eyes closed in a white towelling bathrobe. The room with its massive stonework was narrow and long; an ancient, bulky, carved closet separated the two single beds positioned parallel along the wall.

Julia tiptoed around, got some fresh underwear from her suitcase, and went two steps up into the bathroom to have a shower. Even this had been carved out of the rock. It had a high domed ceiling, lots of bare stonework everywhere and smooth tiling just around the shower, washbasin and toilet.

The water was wonderfully refreshing. Wearing her uniform, she left quietly and went downstairs. She didn't meet anyone, and went outside into the warm afternoon sun.

There weren't many people about at this time of the day. Using the street plan, she paused on the narrow stone terrace in front of the hotel, and then headed towards the dome on the highest point of the town. It didn't seem far away, but the streets twisted and turned. The route wasn't direct; in the end, she orientated herself by following the position of the bell tower, as it soared above everything else.

She reached it, and studied the exterior of the Romanesque cathedral but didn't go inside. It would be part of Roark Ellis's tour tomorrow, and there was no point in seeing everything in advance. She sat down in the shade, on a nearby rough wall, and took in the atmosphere.

She jumped when a deep voice catapulted her out of her musing.

'Taking a look around?'

Roark Ellis was just behind her, and she answered sensibly. 'Yes, it seems a shame to waste the time sleeping. I'm not tired and I'll be busy looking after the guests from now on. I wanted a preview.' She looked ahead towards the cathedral. 'It's pretty impressive, isn't it?'

He looked very relaxed and eyed her pleasantly. 'It was completely restored in the Baroque period and there are some interesting wooden sculptures and a XV century choir. Go inside and look. With your background, you'll probably appreciate it more than most people.'

She smiled. 'I thought about it, but decided to wait until I follow you around tomorrow with the others. I'm sure it will be more interesting to hear your comments than wandering around with a brochure on my own.'

He smiled, and all of a sudden Julia was fully aware of her surroundings, and of him. Silly — but he was a damned attractive man and he was intelligent and a practised intellectual to boot.

'If you're not going inside come and share an espresso with me, in that café over there.'

There was no reason to refuse; it was a perfectly innocent invitation. She nodded and fell into step as they crossed the sunlit square and moved to where large-leafed trees shaded the tables cluttering the pavement outside the small bistro. A waiter came, and he ordered.

'Your brother told me you've been here often?'

'Did he? Yes, I like this region very much, because it's still unknown to most people. This part of Italy was always one of the poorest, and progress still drags its feet. Things have changed a lot in the last couple of years but luckily it still has a lot of its original appeal. Some people don't like this kind of landscape at all, but I do. It's special and steeped in history.'

The waiter arrived and served them their espressos. Julia stirred her cup with a silver spoon and added a little sugar. 'Those mountains we saw on the way, they're the Apennines?'

'Yes, almost two thousand metres high, although we're only roughly four hundred metres here in Matera. The whole vicinity is plastered with history of course, from Greek settlements, via the Romans, through the Middle Ages right up to modern times.'

'I understand why you like it. I read about it before we left and there's enough to keep anyone interested in history busy for years.'

Julia looked at the compelling grey eyes, firm features and confident set of his shoulders. He seemed surprisingly relaxed with her, and her negative thoughts about him slowly began to dissolve. He had a level of confidence and quiet assurance that she liked, even though she could see that behind his civility he was still watchful and wary.

He asked about where she'd studied. The shared coffee break was perfectly harmless and she began to feel comfortable in his company.

He looked at his watch. 'Would you like something else?'

'No thanks, Mr Ellis.' She fumbled in her bag for her purse.

He lifted his hand. 'Don't be silly! I invited you, and an espresso won't break the bank. And please, call me Roark.'

Julia coloured slightly. 'I will, if you call me Julia.'

He nodded.

Julia stood up. 'I'm now going to try to find a post office. I always send my gran a postcard from the places we visit. My parents couldn't care less about postcards, they're happy with the occasional text.' Her eyes twinkled. 'Sometimes the cards arrive a long time after I get back, but Gran doesn't mind. She takes them to show her friends at her bridge club and then sticks them on the wall in the kitchen. She says she looks at them and thinks of me every day when she's having breakfast.'

Roark decided that no one who liked her gran as she did could be disagreeable. She also had an air of calm and self-confidence about her that he liked — even though he'd absolutely no intention of complicating his life with any woman ever again. He watched as she studied the detailed town plan in her hand.

He lifted his hand and the waiter came. Roark paid and got up adding, 'There's a post office not far from here on the via del Corso, and you'll find postcards on sale somewhere along the way.'

Julia thought that he intended to go his own way, but he surprised her when he said, 'I'll take you, if you like. The old part of the city is a bit confusing until you get used to it.'

'Thanks, that'd be great, if it's no bother.'

Roark decided that she was the type of girl who wouldn't settle for a fleeting affair. She didn't flirt; she was friendly, fresh, and intelligent, and probably needed a committed partner who was the so-called love of a lifetime. He thought he'd had that once, but everything had gone wrong — never again. 'No, of course not, otherwise I wouldn't have offered.'

'We have to keep to the itinerary

from tomorrow onwards, but we're free now.' He fitted his stride to hers.

'They seem to be a very nice crowd and no one has complained so far,' she said as they made their way through the streets.

He chuckled. 'Someone will, just wait. Some people actually enjoy having a go at the representatives.'

She wrinkled her nose and smiled.

He continued to chat about the town and he came inside the post office with her to help. On the way out she said, 'Your Italian is very good!'

He shrugged his shoulders. 'I try. A good knowledge of Latin helps with modern Italian.'

The streets were narrow and it would have taken Julia much longer to find her way back alone. The sun was setting and shadows were deepening between the greyish-beige buildings. The temperature was still pleasant, and Julia was impressed by her companion.

When they reached the hotel, she glanced up at the windows and saw

Claudia looking down. The flimsy white curtain twitched and Claudia disappeared without the least acknowledgment.

When she got to their room, Claudia didn't comment on seeing Julia with Roark or ask any questions, so Julia didn't mention how she'd met him. Claudia was putting her things in the closet and Julia noted she'd used up most of the hangers.

Julia unpacked her suitcase, doubling things over the hangers and then pushed her suitcase underneath the bed. She escaped to the bathroom and renewed her make-up. She brushed her ash-blonde hair until it shone, put on more eye make-up than usual, and added a pair of simple pearl earrings. Claudia had already disappeared when she came out again.

Looking at her watch, Julia saw she had a little time before she needed to be in the foyer; dinner was served later than in colder climes. The representatives were expected to be on hand throughout mealtimes, in case someone had a question or a problem.

Julia settled down with a paperback, but her thoughts wandered to her unexpected meeting with Roark Ellis. There was more friendliness behind his serious looks than she ever imagined.

3

The meal was delicious. Julia shared it at a small corner table with two women who were travelling on their own. They were widows and friends, who'd joined forces to spend an informative and enjoyable holiday. They were spritely and animated, obviously delighted at being abroad. Julia heard about their children and grandchildren and their hobbies. She told them a little about herself, and the soft laughter from their table drifted across the rest of the company as Julia told them of some of the unusual and funny things she'd experienced at university.

Claudia looked in their direction suspiciously. The atmosphere gradually relaxed, and people began to talk more freely amongst themselves. Claudia shared a table with Roark, a music director, and a librarian.

After dinner when everyone was enjoying a final glass of wine or some coffee, Claudia got up and adjusted the flowing lines of her chiffon blouse. 'I think, and hope everyone enjoyed our first meal in Italy?' There was a wave of affirmation. 'Good! I've a town plan of Matera for everyone, so if you want to go for a walk after dinner, you're free to do so. Breakfast is from 6.30a.m. here, in this room. We leave on the tour of Matera with Professor Ellis after breakfast at 9a.m. and we'll meet up in the foyer. Please be punctual; we've no intention of waiting for anyone. I think you'll agree that the enjoyment of the whole group shouldn't be spoiled by someone who can't make an effort to be on time.'

There was a murmur of assent.

'You already have the itinerary, so there's no need for me to tell you what's on the agenda for tomorrow. Packed lunches will be provided by the hotel, and we'll be stopping somewhere suitable along the way to enjoy them.

Wear casual clothes and appropriate footwear, please! We hope that you have a restful night. My colleague Julia will be at the hotel this evening, in case you have any questions or problems to solve. Enjoy the evening, and we'll meet again, tomorrow morning in the foyer.'

There was a soft ripple of applause. Julia was surprised that she'd have to hang about the hotel, that had never been necessary before, but she'd already been for a stroll so she didn't feel cheated.

The group drifted out of the dining room. Some went to their rooms, others headed for the entrance, street-plan in hand.

Julia waited for a while until they were all out of sight. No one had a problem. She shrugged, fetched her book and made herself comfortable at one of the small tables on the narrow terrace.

Roark came out after a while and he stopped in front of her.

'Damned to idleness?'

Julia smiled up at his tall figure. 'Oh, I don't mind. I've already been out on an excursion and a couple of hours with a book isn't a punishment!'

'What are you reading?'

Julia held her book aloft. 'Nothing intellectual; the latest John Irving.'

'Not bad! I like his books too.'

He stuck his hands in the pockets of his light chinos. Daylight was fading and the whiteness of his shirt was caught by the lamplight, and it carved hollows in his face. 'I'm going for a stroll, to digest all that food.'

'Um! It was wonderful, wasn't it? Italian food is so variable and tasty. Mountains of calories of course, but the majority of Italians are slim, so there must be a secret behind it somewhere.'

He chuckled. 'Probably.' He seemed almost reluctant to leave. 'I'll see you later.'

He was already on his way down the narrow terrace towards the next roadway, when Claudia came out of the foyer and hurried after him. 'Roark, wait for me!'

She didn't even glance in Julia's direction as she rushed to catch up with his departing silhouette. Julia noted that he didn't slow down. She wondered if he realised that Claudia had set her sights on him.

★ ★ ★

The next day things followed the set plans and Julia enjoyed the walk through the town. They visited the cathedral and took a leisurely walk until it was time to enjoy their sandwich lunch in a shady green square. They visited the archaeological museum in the afternoon and then went on to a visit to a couple of cave churches with religious frescoes.

Roark was an enjoyable, informative guide; he intertwined humorous historical anecdotes with facts. Julia could tell that everyone was interested. He didn't use incomprehensible historical terminology and masses of dates. Julia hung around at the back of the group, listening. She'd changed her opinion about him; Roark Ellis was someone worth knowing.

Walking the hard pavements hewn out of the rocks was tough going. Back at the hotel, everyone dispersed quickly, glad to have a shower and a rest before dinner.

★　★　★

After breakfast next morning, Claudia informed Julia that she'd have to find some supplier for a cheese and wine lunch for the group, somewhere along the way.

Julia had expected it to happen; she thought she might be targeted with the task ever since Claudia mentioned it, back at headquarters, but it wasn't less daunting. Where was she to find cheese and wine suppliers? She borrowed a pile of white tablecloths, some empty Chianti bottles, cutlery, plates and serviettes from the hotel. The coach driver was the same one who'd brought them from the airport. He looked puzzled when Julia handed him the filled cardboard boxes. Julia decided he might be the right person to ask for help.

Enzo was a good-looking, swarthy Italian, and even though he was enamoured of his fiancee Carla, he was still a little captivated by this English girl with her delicate skin and laughing eyes.

'Non problema!' Eyeing Claudia, but talking to Julia, he said, 'When we get to La Trinita, the others will go to the ruins. I'll leave you at a picnic area outside the town and you can get the tables ready. I'll get some local foodstuff from someone I know. Food and wine for roughly twenty-five people, okay? I'll bring it back to the picnic spot and then fetch the others.'

Julia nodded enthusiastically and thanked the patron saint of Matera for sending her Enzo. Claudia had given her a generous amount of money to cover the costs. Enzo talked to someone on his cell phone in machine-gun Italian. A few seconds later, he grinned and gave her a thumbs-up sign.

Julia was immensely relieved, and impulsively hugged him and kissed his cheek. Roark was looking for Enzo and saw them. His brows drew together in a straight line but he didn't comment. Julia coloured slightly, but it had nothing to do with Roark Ellis what she did or with whom. She went to stand near the rear door of the bus for the last of the stragglers. When the bus drew away, Julia leaned back and began to think about table decorations.

They drove to Venosa and walked through the town centre before paying a short visit to the archaeological museum. The bus then dropped the group off at the unfinished monastery of La Trinita, and Enzo took her to the nearby picnic ground. He left her there with her cardboard boxes and said he'd be back within the hour.

He was, and by then Julia had covered the rough tables with the tablecloths, arranged the plates and cutlery, filled the empty bottles with wild flowers and olive twigs, and wound long-stemmed wild flowers around the serviettes. Enzo came laden with heavy baskets and whistled when he saw the arrangement.

'Magnifico!'

He put the baskets on one of the benches and looked at his watch. 'I'll pick them up! Here's the bill and the change. I can take the containers back next time I'm passing.'

Julia nodded. 'I'm so grateful Enzo. I wouldn't have managed on my own; I definitely wouldn't have had any time to decorate the tables.'

Enzo brushed her thanks aside and whistling loudly, he sauntered towards the bus.

Julia shared out the cheeses, sausages, crispy bread, fragrant focaccia and handed round olives, paprika, bunches of fat grapes and huge sun-kissed tomatoes. She positioned full bottles of red and white Chianti at intervals and added bottles of fruit juice and mineral water from the bus.

When people arrived and saw the tables full of Italian fare, the acclaim was unanimous. Everyone was enthusiastic about the impromptu meal.

They had the picnic ground to themselves. The tables were beneath old trees with long branches that provided plenty of shade. No praise passed Claudia's lips. She let her critical glance sweep up and down the tables. Julia didn't care; any employee with a bit of sense should be glad if something was successful but Claudia couldn't be magnanimous about anyone else's efforts.

A few minutes later Roark came to stand near her, a piece of crusty farmhouse bread spread with thick butter in his hand. He bit off a chunk with healthy white teeth. He nodded towards the informal spread. 'Great! The sort of thing people remember long after the holiday is over.'

Julia's cheeks coloured. 'Enzo saved my bacon. I wouldn't have managed without him.'

'But you made it look so appetising,' he enthused. 'You couldn't do quite the same thing in Britain, could you? The weather's too changeable, and we stick to the same kind of food for picnic baskets.'

'That's true. Picnics work perfectly here. Just look at these local cheeses and sausages. I bet you'd never find any of them for sale on the open market, not even in Harrods.'

'I'm going to get some more before it all disappears!' He gave her an arresting smile and headed back to the bustle of satisfied people enjoying an informal lunch in the open air.

If he objected to her kissing Enzo, he seemed to have forgotten it. Julia went to the back of the bus, to help Enzo fetch another case of mineral water for their guests.

4

The people on the tour were all very accomodating, and some of them, like the two widows, seemed to go out of their way to help make her day function well. Julia was feeling satisfied.

They kept to the itinerary and visited churches, hilltop towns and former Greek settlements.

Another picnic lunch was planned. This time Claudia said she'd organise it, and Julia was content to accompany the group and Roark.

Claudia made the mistake of not asking Enzo for help. She went on solitary expeditions to find suitable foodstuff and only used Enzo to transport her about. She copied the idea of tablecloths, china and cutlery, and knew she wouldn't have much time for elaborate table decorations.

The result was okay but unpretentious and they ran out of cheese. Julia tried not to be critical. Claudia had miscalculated badly, and it didn't improve her humour.

Julia sat and ate with the others, making small talk and enjoying the local sausage and fat juicy olives. Claudia hadn't complimented Julia's picnic lunch, so Julia ignored Claudia's efforts too.

These days, Roark was friendly even though he was still a cautious character. He was guarded behind his polite facade but Julia took him as she found him and made no extra demands. She left him to his own thoughts when she felt that was what he wanted and he appreciated that.

Julia found it easy to chat to him when he singled her out for any attention and with the passing of time, he seemed to accept her completely.

After the first day of the tour, Roark moved from the front seat next to the driver to let guests take turns in enjoying a better view of the road. He sat wherever there was a vacant seat. Julia saw that people were anxious to have him as a travelling companion. Once Roark moved away from the front seat, Claudia did too. Usually she shoved herself into the corner of the back seat, ignoring everyone as much as her job allowed. Julia continued to sit next to anyone who was alone.

It had been a warm and interesting day of touring but everyone was glad to be back at the hotel. After dinner, Claudia pleaded a headache and said she was going to bed. Luckily, she forgot to find some fictitious reason to keep Julia in the hotel, so Julia changed into one of the simple cotton dresses she had with her and slipped out, leaving Claudia dozing.

The warmth of the day was gradually slipping into a cooler Italian twilight. It was pleasant to be alone and she had no particular place she wanted to go; she just wandered along the terraces. Julia found it easy to guess where she was, the bell tower was a great help; you could see it everywhere.

After a while, she sat down on one of the walls and pulled her legs up. Resting her chin on her knees and wrapping her arms around her legs, she looked down at the structures and buildings below and watched the lights gradually coming on. Bright stars were also beginning to appear in the black velvet heaven above. It was wonderful to sit in silence and let the mild Italian breezes play with her hair.

People passed; one of them had a scruffy, but happy looking dog that gave her a few wags of his long-haired tail as he passed. A tall dark silhouette was climbing upwards via the tiered pathways from the Sassi on the lower levels. Involuntarily, her heartbeat increased when she realised it was Roark. He was deep in thought, and Julia wondered if he'd pass without registering her. Hands in his pockets, his chin dipped towards his chest, the light wind played with his hair. He walked easily at a steady, moderate pace.

He did notice her, though, and came to a sudden halt. His chin came up and the dark hollows of his face deepened further when he turned from the sparse wall lights towards her.

'Hi Julia! What are you doing here? Haven't you done enough walking for one day?'

She smiled into the dark. 'I could ask you the same question! I just wanted to enjoy some solitary moments in Matera by night.'

'Would you like me to pretend I haven't seen you?'

Julia laughed softly. 'No, of course not. I imagine you welcome some peace and quiet more than I do. I bet you're glad there's no one around who asks how old it is, when it was built or why.' She swung her legs over the edge of the rough wall and sat up straight.

He sat down at her side, resting his hands on the wall at both sides of his hips. 'There are occasionally people who try to pull the rug out from under your feet but they're few and far between. I'm convinced some people read up like mad on the places we target, just to try to show the guide up, if they can.' He smiled.

'Really?' She considered. 'Yes, you're probably right. That teacher from Chester is like that, isn't he?'

She looked sideways at him and wondered what sort of life he normally led. She'd never asked him any personal questions, and he'd never offered much personal information. He was one of the youngest professors she had ever met, and she had no doubt about the quality or extent of his knowledge. He wouldn't be a professor at his age unless he was above average in some way. Julia tried to ignore his presence and concentrate on her surroundings. She turned to look at the town spread out below them. 'Perfect, isn't it?'

He nodded, and they sat silent for a while. The breeze ruffled her dress and messed her hair. Julia felt an urge to let her legs dangle over the wall but instead she half-turned to take in the view. He turned inward too and they met each other's gaze. His dark eyes twinkled in the night. The silence was prolonged. With an unexplainable lump in her throat, she studied his shadowy profile and then they both spoke at once.

'What about . . . '

'What's . . . '

They both gave a soft laugh, and Roark finished his sentence. 'What about a glass of wine? There's a nice little bar just down the road. We have an early start tomorrow, but it would be a good way to end the day.'

Julia came to her feet. 'Yes. I'd like that.'

He got up and put his hand under her elbow. She followed his lead, and they wandered slowly down the hill to a small bar with a couple of tiny tables outside. Coloured lights hung in loose chains along the wall and around a well-loved and well-cared for fig tree. They sat down at one of the tables and Roark ordered them a carafe of wine. It looked black when it arrived, and she held it up to the sparse light to see the red pigmentation.

'Cheers!'

Roark lifted his and repeated. 'Cheers!'

They both took a sip. It was rough on the tongue but fruity and tasted good. Julia was fascinated as she noted how he played with the stem of his glass; he had big hands with slim fingers and neat nails. She realised she was a little enchanted with him, perhaps because he was a professor and, in theory, she was still a student.

'At the interview you said you needed to earn money. I presume it's for a special reason?'

She nodded. 'I need my teaching certificate, so that I can apply for a teaching job. I should have done it straight after my degree, but something got in the way.'

'You're planning to teach? It's not an easy job these days, you know.'

She tilted her head to the side. 'I don't think it ever was. It depends on you and the school. I like children, I always have, and I hope I can instil some enthusiasm into them — if I ever get that far. I don't even know what the course entails yet; I just know I need the qualification.'

'How expensive?'

'I think I need about four thousand pounds.'

'That's quite a lot, if you haven't got a steady job.'

'I'm saving my wages now, and if the job lasts long enough, I'll be able to apply for a course after Christmas.' She put her hand up to her mouth. 'I shouldn't actually be telling you this, should I? You shouldn't know that I'm not planning to be around longer than absolutely necessary.'

He smiled. 'You signed a contract for six months. Keith will hold you to that. If you need to go beyond that time, you have to negotiate with him. It's nothing to do with me.'

'I'm determined to save as fast as I possibly can. I live with my gran at the moment. She won't take anything for my keep, so I can put all of my wages away.'

'And your parents?'

'They live in Chester, but I wanted to be near London, because I thought it would be easier to find work there. My brother is also at university now, so I bet they're glad I'm off their hands at present. My gran is a love, so I feel really comfortable with the situation.'

He nodded thoughtfully and took another sip of wine. 'You mentioned your gran before. She seems to be an important person in your life.'

Julia was surprised he'd remembered. 'She is. She's very active, very independent, very supportive, and lovely. I hope I can pay her back one day, and I don't mean financially.' Julia didn't have enough courage to ask him personal questions. She didn't even know if he was married; someone like him probably was. 'I presume that you like your work?'

'Yes. It's very rewarding.'

'And you live in London?'

He hesitated. 'Yes, I have a flat, not far from Birbeck, and I bought a small holiday home down on the Gower recently. That's where we come from originally.'

'I presumed you were a one hundred per cent Englishman.'

'Is there such a thing these days? Ellis is an ancient Welsh name.'

She was puzzled. 'But Roark is . . . '

He explained. 'Gaelic. My mother read the name in a book when I was on the way. She liked it. Names often fascinate people, don't they? Keith spent ages tracing our family tree when he was much younger.'

'And? Did he make any interesting findings?'

'Yes, we had a harp-player at the courts of one of the Welsh Princes, bowmen who fought for the English crown in the Middle Ages. A travelling medicine man with dubious cures that got him into trouble with the law, and someone mixed up in the Chartist

Movement who was deported to Australia. He came back to England after twenty years and helped to found unions in the coal mines.'

'I'm impressed!'

'Don't be.' He chuckled. 'The majority of them led very humdrum existences. I bet you'd be equally surprised if someone dug back into your family's history.'

'We'd probably uncover highway men, murderers, thugs and ruffians.'

There was music playing softly in the background, and the soft murmur of other people at the nearby tables made it an evening to remember.

He shared the remaining wine between the two glasses, leaned back and took a generous gulp from his own glass. He looked down at his wristwatch. 'We have an early start tomorrow; we'd better head back to the hotel.'

Julia took another sip, and stood up. He went indoors to pay for the wine and she sauntered slowly in the direction they'd come from. He caught up with her. They were silent most of the way back. Just outside the hotel, he turned to face her and, to her surprise, he kissed her on her cheek. 'Have a good night's sleep.'

Finding her voice at last, she smiled and said, 'Thanks for the wine and the same to you.' She turned away and went inside.

Roark stood for a moment, astonished at himself, that he'd simply followed an instinct and kissed her like that. Even though it was an innocent kiss, it was a stupid move. Luckily, she was a sensible woman; she wouldn't place too much importance on it. He'd better keep a friendly but definite distance from now on, to make sure that she didn't think he had something else in mind.

Climbing the red-carpeted stairs, Julia touched her cheek. He was just being friendly, she realised that, but somehow she wished he hadn't kissed her. It wakened all kinds of silly possibilities in her mind, and she didn't want complications in her life. They were just ships that were passing in the night.

When she reached their room, Claudia was sitting on the edge of her bed; she looked irritated. Had she been watching from the window again and seen her and Roark coming back? Julia said a quick hello, and began to get ready for bed. Taking her pyjamas from under her pillow, she changed in the bathroom and cleaned her teeth. She was looking out clothes for the next day when Claudia broke the silence.

'It won't do you any good.'

Julia looked up in surprise. 'Pardon?'

'Chasing Roark — it won't do you any good.' Claudia shrugged. 'You might catch him for a quick affair, but you'll end up the same as all the women he's known and discarded, since his wife left him.'

The air seemed to leave Julia's lungs and she must have looked like a fish out of water but she managed to answer. 'Sorry, I don't know what you mean, or what you are talking about.'

Claudia got up and went to lean on the window-sill. 'Roark's wife cheated on him almost from the day they got married. It took him three years to admit finally that all the hints he'd received from various people were true, and it was time to wrap things up. It shouldn't have affected his professional standing, but it did; all the gossip had negative effects and he changed universities once the divorce was through.'

Julia was feeling too sorry for Roark to wonder why Claudia was telling her all this. She'd never talked to her about anything personal ever since they'd met.

Claudia's voice droned on. 'His wife came from South Africa, and when he finally confronted her, she just packed her bags and left. I really think that he didn't know what was going on for a long time. Roark was bound up in his work and he trusted her. Naturally, he doesn't trust any woman any more. He's had affairs, yes; but a real love affair, no. Don't build your hopes up too high, not unless you'll be satisfied with a quick trip between the sheets and empty arms afterwards.'

Julia was still absorbing Claudia's information but she managed to reply. 'I'm not hoping for any kind of relationship. Roark is polite and kind to me. I like him, but I'm not looking for more, and I'm sure he isn't either. Why are you telling me this?'

Claudia turned to face her, with a bland expression and unreadable eyes. 'Because I thought you should know; I don't want you to get hurt.'

Julia didn't believe her, but didn't say so. Probably the real reason was that Claudia was after Roark herself. She was always trying to be with him and keep him apart from anyone else. If Claudia knew that Roark wasn't looking for a serious relationship, and felt she had to 'warn' Julia, why was she still pursuing him herself? Either she was head over heels in love with him and was trying to prevent any rivalry, or she hoped to isolate him from other women because she was hoping for a casual affair. Somehow, Julia thought that Claudia underestimated his intelligence and his determination. He may have made a mistake about a woman once, but she doubted if he'd make a mistake again. If he wanted an affair, he'd make it plain enough; if he didn't she wouldn't have a chance.

Julia didn't understand why Claudia was so alarmed about Julia's position. Claudia was welcome to him, if she could get him. Mike had made her mistrustful and wary of men and she was glad she was free. She'd never be so gullible again or make the same mistake twice.

She made no effort to continue the conversation. She turned away, closed the wardrobe, and was glad the cupboard was a solid barrier between them. Julia got into bed and thumped her pillow. She couldn't see Claudia any more and was glad. She put out her light and Claudia did too. The room was blanketed in darkness and Julia stared up into the gloom.

She'd have felt happier if Claudia hadn't told her about Roark but she didn't think less of him after what she'd heard. She sympathised, because no matter whose fault it had been, she was sure he was the kind of character who appeared to be very strong — but had chinks in his armour just like anyone else.

Despite her efforts to forget everything and get some sleep, she couldn't and she now wished Claudia had kept the information to herself. As she tossed and turned, Julia's thoughts tumbled out of control. Even if Roark was free, he met women every day of his life, professionally and socially; there was nothing above the ordinary about Julia Radford. It took some time until she fell into an uneasy slumber.

5

The rest of the tour went off without a hitch. There were no other opportunities for quiet solitary talks with Roark, and Julia didn't know if she was pleased or sorry. She just knew that she liked him. She thought highly of how he handled people, he remained friendly without giving too much of himself. Some academics she knew lived in a world of their own and had difficulties relating to everyday people.

Roark managed to give information mixed up with chitchat about people's ordinary living conditions, famous personalities of that age, or about other comparable nations of the same era. Their guests had time to think and absorb, and he was always prepared to answer anyone's questions patiently.

Julia couldn't understand that his ex-wife wanted someone else. Overall, he was a very considerate and likeable man. She could tell the vast majority of tour members thought so too. His ex-wife must have had some other reason to want someone else.

When they got back to Gatwick, they received effusive thanks from everyone. Julia, Claudia and Roark waited until the final one had departed and had been swallowed up by the bustle of the airport.

Roark stuck out his hand. 'Bye, Julia! Good luck with your next tour, and on eventually achieving your goal.'

Julia shook his hand; it felt warm. She had conflicting emotions. Now that they were parting, she admitted that her thoughts about him were sometimes uncontrolled, and she was being very, very stupid. She was slightly starstruck. 'Bye! Thanks for all your interesting talks and information. I enjoyed the tour almost as much as the people who paid to be on it.'

He smiled and Julia was mesmerised by his dark eyes and their hidden expression. She turned quickly to Claudia. 'I'll see you at head office?'

Claudia answered politely. 'Yes, if I'm not there when you arrive, just leave everything on my desk and tell Joel that it's there.'

Julia wondered why Claudia couldn't be magnanimous for once and save her a trip to the office by taking the documentation off her hands now. She grabbed the handle of her trolley-bag and turned away. As she was leaving she heard Claudia saying, 'We can share a taxi into town Roark, can't we? You go past my place anyway.'

Julia began to fight her way through the airport jostle to the bus stop.

* * *

Three other tours followed, and Julia tried not to think about Roark. The first tour was through the Loire valley. It was lovely and interesting; the first time Julia had been there. The second tour was a repeat of the one she'd already been on, along the border between France and Germany. It wasn't so interesting a second time around, even though it went without a hitch. The third tour took her to Paris, Versailles and Fontainebleau.

She'd been to Paris twice before — once on her own, and once with the company to learn the ropes. Versailles and Fontainebleau were new to her.

When she got back, there was an invitation to a company party; Keith was celebrating his fortieth birthday. She was free and Gran said she should 'wear her best frock and go'. She did, even though she still didn't know many faces at headquarters. The nature of her job meant she was either coming, or going.

Julia wore a favourite white shift dress and high heels. Her skin had an attractive pale bronze sheen from being outdoors so much. When she arrived, she edged across to Joel; she knew him because he worked hand-in-hand with Claudia.

He introduced her to some others gathered near him and Julia was glad to stand around and be part of a crowd, even if she didn't know any of them.

After a while, Keith arrived with his secretary. He made a hillarious speech about 'growing older' and thanked them for the collective present of an expensive fountain pen and pencil set. Champagne did the rounds, and a buffet was laid out on tables along one of the walls.

Julia had been expecting to see Claudia, but there was no sign of her. Her curiosity got the better of her. She asked Joel. 'Where's Claudia?'

He shrugged. 'I don't know, but I think there's been some kind of rumpus. I know that she went to Keith's office sometime yesterday morning and she came back with a face like thunder. She threw papers around, collected some stuff from the drawers, and went off without any explanation. She's always been an explosive character, so I didn't pay too much attention, but I'm beginning to wonder if there was more to it than meets the eye. Claudia would never intentionally miss a do like this.'

'Perhaps something went wrong on one of the tours, and she was hauled over the coals for it?'

He shook his head. 'I don't think so. That kind of blunder is soon general knowledge. I checked the papers she'd thrown around after she'd left. Funnily enough, it was the itinerary for your next tour, something that hasn't even taken place yet, so I don't know what it was about. We'll hear in due course, no doubt. How did your last tour go? Any problems?'

Julia was glad to talk business. Someone eventually dragged him away, so when she circled Julia was pleased to find the tour assistant she'd accompanied to Paris again. When Julia caught Keith's eye, she lifted her glass, and he raised his in acknowledgement.

The other girl said, 'I won't be staying very long. I just felt I had to show face, but . . . '

Julia smiled. 'I know what you mean. I'm only putting in an obligatory appearance too. When I leave, no one will even notice I've been. Joel knows me, but I don't know many of the others.'

Some minutes later, they joined the leisurely crowd who were gathering to congratulate Keith. When it was their turn, Julia held out her hand and said, 'Happy Birthday!'

Keith Ellis smiled warmly. 'Thank you Julia. I'm glad you came. You're one of our more recent employees, but every single person, past or present, is important in this place.'

Julia laughed softly. 'I'm a very small cog in the machine, but I enjoy the work very much.'

'Good! We must have a proper talk one day soon. Talk about the future.'

Julia was glad it wasn't going to be now. She was almost sure that she'd reach her saving goal by the end of this contract; she wanted to move on. She did enjoy the work — it was a wonderful way to see foreign places, but she didn't want to be side-tracked. She was here to save money for a teaching certificate. Julia just nodded and made room for the next person in the straggling row forming behind her.

Her colleague from the Paris trip was waiting for her, and they took a couple of bits and bobs from the buffet and another glass of champagne. A couple of minutes later they decided they'd been there long enough to satisfy necessity. They withdrew quietly, and parted outside, going in opposite directions. The road was lined with beautiful large-leafed lime trees and it was relatively quiet. Julia strolled on, wondering if she'd do some window-shopping, or just catch the next train home.

She looked up and her heart skipped a beat when she saw Roark striding energetically towards her. When he saw her, he seemed to hesitate for a fraction of a second too but he came on and halted in front of her.

It had only been a couple of weeks,

but Julia admitted it seemed like an eternity, and she realised she'd missed seeing him. She smiled nervously. 'Hello Roark!'

'Hello! Going already? I expected to see you at the party.' He noticed that her hair was clipped back, and liked it.

'Yes, I've already had my share of the champagne and appetizers. I was just deciding whether to do something else with the afternoon, or just go home.' She added, 'I still have three free days before the next tour leaves.'

He smiled and stuck his hand deep in his pocket. He looked smart in a loose fitting grey suit and formal tie. The suit was probably a lot more expensive than anyone would imagine.

'Pity! I hoped we might have a chat, but that's the punishment I get for turning up late.'

She tilted her head to the side and felt ridiculously pleased to see him. 'It probably would have been even more punishment if I'd stayed — I might have talked your ears off about all the tours I've been on since we last met.'

He eyed her slowly and deliberately. 'I don't honestly think that would have been a punishment.'

She coloured and wished she was sophisticated enough to parry his words with something just as trivial.

He continued. 'We'll be seeing each other soon anyway?'

Puzzled, Julia looked and waited. 'Really?'

'Basilicata?'

Julia shrugged her shoulders; she was still puzzled.

'Your next-but-one tour is Basilicata, and I'm lecturer again.'

The words sent her pulse spinning and she felt slightly confused and disorientated. 'I didn't know. Claudia hasn't mentioned it. I saw her at the end of last week, when I handed in the stuff from the last tour. I'm surprised she didn't tell me.'

'No doubt you haven't heard the news. Claudia is officially no longer with the company.'

Feeling mildly shocked, she didn't like to ask why; instead she just commented, 'Isn't she? No, I didn't. Who's coming with us this time?'

'No one. As far as I know, it's just you and me and eighteen guests.'

If she'd been standing on a rug, Julia would have sworn someone had pulled it from under her feet at that moment. She tried to force her confused thoughts into order. She swallowed hard and said, 'Oh! That'll be nice!'

He gave her one of his irresistible smiles and her knees felt weak. How stupid! How ridiculous! How dangerous!

'We have always managed with just one lecturer and one representative on our tours, and I told Keith so when Claudia suggested coming again.' The dark eyebrows slanted and pulled into a frown. 'I don't even understand why Claudia trailed along last time. It was totally unnecessary and an extra expense the company could have done without.'

Julia guessed why, but didn't comment. She nodded like an automaton instead, and wondered why she felt so bewildered. She tried to think of something else to talk about, something sensible to say. 'Keith looks a lot younger than forty, doesn't he?'

'Put that down to a caring wife and the right attitude.'

'I didn't know he was married.'

His brows arched mischievously and then he looked thoughtful. 'Most employees know all the ins and outs about their boss — especially as Likely Prospect is a fairly small concern.'

'Oh, it's not that I'm disinterested, but I'm seldom at headquarters. Are you his younger brother?'

'Yes, by five years, and we have a sister who is younger still — and she has absolutely nothing to do with the company, thank heavens.'

Julia was torn in two directions, wanting to linger, and wanting to get away. She was surprised by the effect he was having on her. She thought her interest was casual, but it wasn't. She tipped her head towards the offices. 'If you don't get a move on, you'll miss out on the buffet. They were all beginning to raid it when I left.'

He offered her a sudden smile that left her insides tingling.

'In that case, see you in a fortnight's time. Where are you going on the tour beforehand?'

'At home this time. We're touring some of Capability Brown's gardens. I'm just praying we don't have bad luck with the weather. I'm taking a mac and wellingtons just in case!'

A smile ruffled his mouth. 'I'll keep my fingers crossed for you. Enjoy the rest of the day. See you soon.'

Julia nodded and he moved off. She watched him walk the short distance to the entrance, and how he paused at the top of the steps to look back in her direction again. She waved briefly, and then she went on her way with an added spring in her step.

★ ★ ★

A fortnight later, with heart beating faster than usual, she waited at the meeting point in Gatwick as the tour members began to trickle in. Most of them were couples, but there were some unattached females and one unattached younger man. He was paying a great deal of attention to a woman of roughly the same age. Her jewellery tinkled, her expensive perfume drifted in clouds and her real leather suitcases put everyone else's luggage to shame. Julia checked off people's names as they arrived.

The moneyed woman eyed her smugly. 'I'm Myra Montague.'

Julia ticked her off the list and automatically gave her a smile. 'Thank you Ms Montague. Here's your ticket. We'll be checking-in as soon as I know everyone is here.'

'I hope we won't be hanging around waiting for late comers?'

'Most people are here already. We'll

85

be able to check-in very soon. We always keep an eye on the clock, but there's plenty of time yet.' Julia turned to the man hovering at Myra's side. 'And you are?'

He gave her a well-practised and measured smile. He was exceedingly good-looking, tall, debonair, with blue eyes and blond hair combed casually to one side. 'Lance Meredith.'

Julia made another tick and handed him his ticket. 'I hope you'll enjoy your trip with us.'

Eyeing her with a knowing glance, he said, 'I'm sure I will.'

Julia sighed to herself. Oh Lord, she hoped he wasn't going to be another budding Casanova!

Myra Montague didn't miss the exchange either. She called him to heel. 'Get me a copy of Vogue to read on the plane, Lance.' Casually she handed him a ten pound note, knowing she'd get no change back. Lance pocketed it and looked around for the nearest news-agent.

Julia wondered where Roark was; it wasn't like him to be late. She continued handing out tickets and ticking off the names. To her relief, she saw his long, lean form pulling his case, coming towards them. When he reached her he said, 'Sorry! The taxi got stuck in a traffic jam.'

His ruggedly handsome face was familiar now, but there was a tingling in the pit of her stomach when she smiled and said, 'Still plenty of time.'

Manoeuvring his case to the side, he glanced at the assembled guests. 'Can I help? Is everyone here?'

She checked the list again. 'Only one couple missing. Reverend and Mrs Walter from Uxminster.'

He gave her a mischievous smile. 'No need to worry about them. Higher authorities will be watching over them.'

A few minutes later, a middle-aged, flustered couple came hurrying towards them pulling bulging suitcases behind them. The man took out a handkerchief from his pocket and moped his brow.

His wife explained. 'Awfully sorry, we intended to be here ages ago, but the bus was stuck in a traffic jam — a lorry overturned on the motorway and blocked one of the lanes. It was chaos.'

Julia smiled. 'It's alright, you're still on time. Please don't worry. Mr and Mrs Walter, right?'

He nodded. Julia handed him the ticket. Then she turned to the whole group who were more or less all within distance. 'Ladies and gentlemen, the group is complete. My name is Julia Radford; please call me Julia. This is our accompanying lecturer Professor Roark Ellis. We can now make our way to the check-in counter. Please have your passports ready and remember the strict safety regulations. Also, remember the flight is due to take off at 12.30p.m. and we will be boarding roughly half an hour before then, so keep an eye on the clock and be at the correct departure gate in plenty of time. I hope we'll all have an enjoyable tour, and I welcome you in the name of Likely Prospects.

That's all for now. I'll see you all in the departure lounge.' There was a soft round of applause and they began to disperse quickly in the direction of the check-in desk.

Julia and Roark stood back and let them storm ahead. She gave him a knowing smile and he answered with an expressive look.

'It's amazing isn't it? You'd think they had to fight for a seat. Surely they can figure out that the company books a block of seats?' he said.

'I don't think so. Most just believe it's like any other plane trip — where they have a choice of where they want to sit when they check-in.' She grabbed the handle of the suitcase trolley. 'Let's join them.'

He nodded perfunctorily and grabbed his. He stood over her as they waited in line, and he told her about his taxi's hold-up. They edged forward to the counter. 'I'm looking forward to Basilicata, aren't you?'

She looked up at him. 'Yes, but I'm

on my own this time; I have all the responsibility. Last time Claudia held all the strings.'

'You'll cope. You've proved that you can on all the other tours you've managed. Claudia asked to come but I told Keith we'd manage on our own.' Julia's mouth opened slightly, but she didn't reply. He went on. 'Claudia got in a temper and in the end Keith told her to look for another job.'

Feeling a little surprised, Julia said, 'Claudia and I didn't get on very well.'

He nodded. 'I noticed.'

'But it was silly to pressure her boss.'

He stood motionless. 'It's not a good idea for any employee to hassle their employer unless there's a genuine reason. A boss has to listen to suggestions and ideas, but you stop being an employer if your employees think they have the final say. My brother is fairly flexible, but once he digs in his heels . . . '

He didn't offer any more explanations, and Julia didn't ask for any.

They'd reached the head of the queue and had to concentrate on other things. The moment passed, and Julia was glad. Perhaps Claudia hoped another tour would bring things to a head between herself and Roark.

Once they were through passport and customs control, they strolled slowly towards the departure gate.

'How did the Capability Brown tour go off? Did you need the wellies?'

Feeling light-hearted with the knowledge that she and Roark were a team for the next two weeks, she grinned. 'It was good! I wore the wellies a couple of times. We had one day of non-stop rain, but I'd walked around so many gardens by then, I was content to watch them venture forth without me with their umbrellas unfurled. I spent the time in the tearoom. Some of the gardens were in stately homes but others were belonging to houses that were not open to the general public. One place is now a boarding school. I loved Burghley, and Sherborne Castle.' She tilted her head to the side and her eyes sparkled when she said, 'This job certainly widens one's horizons. I've learned lots about gardens I never knew before.'

He looked across. 'Planning to redesign any?'

'As a matter of fact . . . I did wonder if a rose trellis would look good against my gran's wall. It gets a lot of sun, and I've discovered that roses love the sun.' She laughed.

He flung his arm companionably around her shoulder. 'Have you visited the Acropolis yet?'

She shook her head.

He leaned forward and lowered his voice. 'Just as well — you'd probably want to put up an antique frieze around the shed! Poor Gran! Let's go and have a cup of coffee; we've plenty of time.' He turned her in the direction of a nearby bistro.

She felt a warm glow. She felt good that she was going to spend a fortnight with Roark at her side; what could possibly be better?

6

Enzo was there to meet them again, and they drove to the same hotel in Matera. Julia found that settling people was a bit more hectic because she was alone, but Roark helped, and it was soon sorted out. She had a smaller room to herself and found she could look out over the tops of nearby houses into the distant countryside. If anything, the domed room and its tiny bathroom were even nicer than last time. Julia also knew that the feeling was mainly because Claudia wasn't around any more.

The room was pleasantly cool. She started to sort out the paperwork and put it in appropriate tidy piles and into a banded order. She had the habit of sorting out receipts and the other paperwork as soon as they cropped up. It had to be handed in when she got back, so if she kept it up-to-date as she went along, she had less work at the end of the tour.

She was distracted for a moment or two when she looked out of the open window across the housetops to the sun-drenched Italian countryside beyond. Despite the time of year, the temperatures were still mild in comparison to home. Automatically she thought about the last time she'd been in Matera and how she'd met Roark up by the cathedral on her very first outing.

She reminded herself that she didn't intend to build castles in the air about Roark Ellis, and she wasn't going to mastermind 'chance' meetings with him like Claudia probably had. He wasn't looking for attention, and neither was she. The tour and its success was their sole concern. She brushed silly thoughts aside and concentrated on the paperwork spread out over the bedcovers.

* * *

The daily excursions didn't visit the same places of interest she'd seen first time round. Sitting next to him in the bus the following morning, and glancing now and then at the passing scenery, Julia asked, 'Wouldn't it be easier for you to go to the same places?'

'No, because I'd get very bored. There's so much history in this area, it'd be a shame to concentrate on the same things every time. I work out a rough list of things I think will be worth visiting, give it to the people at head office, and they figure out the best route. Once that's settled they begin to look for restaurants, and the most picturesque routes etc.'

She was intensely aware of his physical nearness and she enjoyed the closeness. She offered him a peppermint but he refused, lifting the microphone as his excuse. She glanced across and said, 'But it means you need to have a lot more knowledge at hand, doesn't it?'

'The basic history is the same for the

whole area even though we go to other places. I have to find out the details of anything we view, but that only means gathering facts and trying to remember them at the right place on the right day.' He leaned to the side and their shoulders touched. He smiled and muttered, 'I always have a list of details for the day in my pocket — in case I get a complete blank, but luckily I haven't needed it so far.'

She watched the bus pass through a small herd of unruly goats being driven along by their owner. 'Well, everyone is always very impressed, so you must have a very good memory.'

'I do, in fact it's almost photogenic. It helped me get through exams in school, and university, and it stands me in good stead in my present job too. If you've a good memory, you have a head's start.' He switched on the microphone and gave a running commentary about a fortress they could see in the distance and switched it off again.

'I wish I had a photogenic memory. I

have to swat and swat for exams. Even then I have trouble remembering what I've actually learned if I start learning too soon before an exam.'

He gave her a good-humoured smile. 'You're not alone there. Not many people are as lucky as I am. It's just a godsend.'

Julia glanced out of the window and back at his face when he continued.

'I don't think that I've actually ever had the same visitor to the same tour twice, but they'd see something different each time with me.'

'I did a tour of the French-German border recently, and we went to exactly the same places. I didn't enjoy it so much the second time around,' she added thoughtfully. 'I'm surprised you find the time to do these tours.'

'I have a very understanding dean, a shared secretary who can organise very efficiently, and I usually have some marking in my suitcase, so I'm not completely deserting my responsibilities. I always enjoy taking a tour if it's possible. It's a kind of working holiday. My students are probably glad to see the back of me for a while.'

Being with him for the greater part of the day made her aware how easily he influenced her emotions and attitude. A voice warned somewhere in the background; that worried her. Sometimes she was almost glad when she had to attend to other things when they stopped somewhere. It was like Annie Lennox's song — she was walking on broken glass. She liked him and enjoyed being with him very much, but she didn't want to end up liking him too much.

Julia usually stood at the back when they viewed something. She noticed how quickly people gathered round Roark and how well he handled them and made his talk entertaining. He still kept an air of reserve about him and managed politely to resist any attempt anyone made to monopolise him. He seemed more relaxed with her, but she tried not to place too much importance on the camaraderie they shared.

Two of the single women had paired up during the tour, and Julia could see they were glad to have someone else to relate to; travelling alone wasn't always enjoyable, unless you were a person who liked solitude. The middle-aged older one was very outgoing. It didn't take her long until she told Julia that she was a widow and that her husband had been a rich industrialist. Her main reason for coming was to get out of the monotone experience of her present daily life.

She wasn't particularly interested in history, didn't like walking much, and was more interested in the scenery, the company, and the food. She also told Julia that the other single woman with a very pasty, sad-looking face was a recent divorcee. She'd been married nineteen years, helped her husband to build up a successful PR business and then found out that he'd been spending weekends with girlfriends in various hotels when he told her he was on business. Julia felt sympathetic but she didn't comment. It wasn't her job to listen to gossip.

During the evening meal, she alternated between sitting at Roark's table and the table of the two women — Mrs Lawson, and her divorcee friend, Susan Harker. All the other people on the tour were couples, except Myra Montague and Lance Meredith. They'd insisted on a table on their own from the start but no one minded. Myra wasn't friendly, and Lance was her toy-boy. Julia wondered why they'd chosen this kind of holiday; an expensive cruise in the sun-drenched Caribbean was more likely their kind of scene.

After dinner, she and Roark were sitting outside on the narrow terrace with a glass of the local red wine. The sun had faded; it was cool but not cold. Julia wrapped her arms around her light cardigan, gave into temptation, and leaned back to enjoy Roark's company. He rested a foot on the rim of a nearby terracotta plant pot, and rested the other on the ground. He looked at ease and comfortable.

'One of those women you sometimes join for dinner looks pretty miserable,' Roark remarked.

She leaned forward and took her glass. 'You mean the younger one of the two? Susan Harker?' He nodded. 'Yes. I gather that she's a recent divorcee, and I expect she hasn't quite adjusted to the situation yet. I haven't talked to her about it personally. I only know what Mrs Lawson has told me.'

Julia had the impression that he stiffened slightly. He was silent for a moment and then picked up his glass, twirling the ruby liquid around, before he took a quick gulp. 'Oh, I see! Divorce does pull you down.'

He didn't say he was speaking from experience, so Julia ploughed on. She wasn't going to pussyfoot around the subject, she was being careful, but she couldn't pretend. 'Apparently, she worked hard to build up a profitable business with him, and he cheated on her. I think Mrs Lawson said they'd been married nineteen years.'

Roark stared ahead. 'Um!' He adjusted his position, leaned forward slightly and rested his arms on his thighs. He played with the glass in his hand. 'I was divorced a couple of years ago; it knocks you about. Divorce confuses you and makes you feel very guilty.'

Julia swallowed a lump in her throat. 'Does it? If a marriage is on the rocks and it's not your fault, it's better to split up and go your own way, though, isn't it?'

There was a hard edge to his voice. 'Ha! There speaks someone who hasn't been married. It isn't always so cut and dried.'

She held her breath for a moment, didn't trust herself to speak, but then said, 'I'm sure it isn't. I'm sure that the vast majority of people who marry want it to last forever, or at least that's what they should want when they start out. However, sometimes circumstances change, and people change. It's very easy for people to drift apart these days; too many diversions, too many temptations and the grass always looks greener on the other side of the hill.'

His forehead was furrowed and his lips were thin lines when he spoke. 'You sound very worldly wise and experienced for someone of your age.'

She bit her lip. 'Do I? I know it's not exactly the same but I wouldn't be here today if a relationship of mine hadn't gone wrong. I know how everything can fall apart overnight. I also know a marriage can survive and last a lifetime — if you choose the right person. You probably have to work at making a marriage work. If your job, other people, or something else is more important, you're on the downward slope. I think a marriage needs understanding, the will to compromise, loyalty and love.'

'Everyone believes in those things, don't they? Things still go wrong.'

She leaned back, toying with her glass, not daring to look at him. 'Some people can't be faithful; it's not in their nature. Some can't compromise and they're incapable of showing understanding for their partner's point of view. People like that shouldn't get married in the first place; they're only deceiving themselves.' Julia didn't know if she was annoying, or hurting him, but she had to say what she thought.

'But no one thinks about love going wrong when they fall in love, do they?' he said.

She shrugged. 'That depends on previous experiences and individual hopes and dreams, doesn't it? When you're young, you see everything through rose-coloured glasses, but disappointment teaches us not to be bowled over by the kind of love that's only based on physical attraction. I've now learned that I could never accept unfaithfulness or live with someone who shows no understanding of what I'm aiming for in life. Marriage is a partnership, not a one-way street. Marriage is a signal to tell the rest of the world how serious you are about the other person, isn't it? If you're not sure, people just live together, but if you live together for a long time but don't take the final step, it's almost a confession that you are expecting things to go wrong, that you're not one hundred per cent sure. I never used to think like that, but I do now.'

The chair creaked under his weight. 'Lots of people live together for purely legal reasons, or because they don't believe in being packed into archaic social structures.'

Julia laughed softly. 'I know, it probably sound crazy. Most people of my age don't see there is anything wrong with marrying for all the wrong reasons. I bet lots of girls get caught up in all the rigmarole of a fancy wedding and forget to ask themselves if the man is really right for them and if they'll be able to stay with him for life.'

His voice was cold and exact. 'When my ex-wife and I married, she wasn't much older than you are now. We were at university together. I decided to stick with academics and she moved into industry to work in communications. We didn't think anything would change — but it did. University was studies and enjoying life, and not thinking about tomorrow or next year. After we married, my wife decided brand names, the right friends, the right circles were the most important things in life. She didn't want children either, something I'd always taken for granted but never discussed. I didn't like the people she went around with, what they did, or how they did it. In my eyes, she changed from a carefree girl into a materialistic woman. When she decided there was nothing wrong in spending time in other men's beds, I decided I'd had enough.' He emptied his glass and set it down with a plonk. He filled it again from the carafe and offered the jug in her direction.

She saw the hurt in his eyes. She shook her head. She showed him that her glass was still almost full. 'Then divorce was right for you. Perhaps she was too young, and the two of you were basically always too different, wanted different things from life from the very beginning. Perhaps serious problems were pre-programmed. Perhaps you'll both be happier with someone else one day.'

He answered determinedly. 'I have no intention of making the same mistake again. We sometimes pay a high price for wanting to be happy.'

'You make it sound as if happiness is a weakness to be avoided at all costs. It isn't. Happiness is a fundamental human need; we all need to be happy sometimes. It doesn't have to be non-stop, but if you feel miserable all the time, it affects the way your life functions. You can find a kind of happiness in friendship, or fulfilling work, but nothing beats finding some-one special to be happy with in a unique relationship for life. Just because you made a wrong choice once doesn't mean you'll never find someone else and be happy with them, does it?'

He eyed her silently and got up. 'I'm extremely sceptical about that. I can tell you've thought a lot about what you want and I hope you find the right one. Marriage didn't work for me, and I still wonder if it was my fault.' He ran his hand over his face and got up abruptly. 'I'm going for a walk before I turn in. See you tomorrow.' He lifted a hand, and without giving her a chance to comment further, he strode off quickly in the direction of the main road.

Julia sat still and pulled the cardigan around tighter. She wished she'd pussyfooted around the conversation about divorce now. She reasoned that she wasn't the first person he'd talked to about it. Even if she ignored it, other people wouldn't. Someone, somewhere, sometime would bring it up. He was obviously still very sensitive about what had happened, and he probably wanted to avoid the subject, but that wouldn't help him to put it behind him and move on. She got up and went indoors, leaving the cool wind rippling across the surface of the wine glasses and the empty carafe on the table.

* * *

The next couple of days went as planned. Roark was as friendly as ever; she didn't notice any change between them, but there was an even stronger air of isolation about him when he thought he was unobserved. Julia didn't make a special effort to join him, during the day or after the evening meal, but she didn't avoid him either. They were generally with one of the group when they were together and that made things easier. They sat side by side in the bus, but he seemed to give more information than usual as they travelled along. Julia buried herself in her own thoughts while watching the passing scenery.

With just two days of the tour left, they were due to visit a late 12th century church rich in frescoes, before going on to Metaponto, an early Greek settlement on the coast. When they arrived at the town, they went to look at the Temple of Hera with its fifteen remaining Doric columns and Roark took them through the charts in the museum illustrating its importance to the region.

Julia and Enzo spent the time preparing a picnic lunch with local fare at a nearby picnic area. Julia decorated the tables with local wild flowers, olives and wine again, becoming more confident and expert at getting it just right. Everyone was enthusiastic about the results and also the food.

The afternoon was free for everyone to spend on the beach, or to walk in the nearby coastal pine and eucalyptus woods. Nearly everyone opted for the beach. The fine sand was golden and there was 35 kilometres of beach, so there was no danger of overcrowding. After emphasising where and when they had to meet up again, Julia watched people as they began to drift off in various directions.

Some had made tentative friendships and they stayed together. Myra strode off in the direction of the crystal-clear water, and Lance fought his way after her, laden with various bags and some beach towels.

Julia glanced in Roark's direction. He was leaning against a nearby fence, talking to Enzo. Julia finished clearing away the remains of the lunch, and Susan and Mrs Lawson helped. 'Thanks! That was kind of you.' Dumping the boxes near the boot of the bus, she straightened up. 'What are you two going to do?'

Mrs Lawson looked undecided. 'I'd love to sit on the sand, but I get a sun allergy if I stay in direct sunshine for too long. Susan and I are going for a walk instead.'

Seeing a chance to avoid too much time with Roark, Julia said, 'I'd like to come, if you don't mind? There's a pathway just behind us, and Enzo says it just wanders straight on and eventually ends up near some hilly farms, not far from here. We could go as far as time allows us.'

Mrs Lawson looked pleased, and Susan was evidently glad that she'd have some company. Julia fetched them some mineral water, and with a wave in the direction to Roark and Enzo, she pointed down the pathway to show them where they were going. The three of them set off.

It was shady and there was a wonderful smell of pine and eucalyptus in the air. 'By gum! This is good for the lungs. Do them a world of good this will,' said Mrs Lawson.

Julia relaxed and so did Susan. They walked in comfortable silence through the dappled pathway. Eventually the vegetation thinned and the road grew rougher. Fences and walls began to edge the pathway, and the fields were full of neglected and abandoned plants.

After a while, they noticed a farm building on the side of a hill further on, and decided to stop for a rest. They went through a rusting gate and towards a group of shady trees in the middle of a field with waist-high plants and weeds. Insects buzzed and swooped, but they weren't aggressive and the grass thinned out as they neared the thick-trunked trees.

Mrs Lawson threw herself down, looking for the most comfortable position. Susan sat down with her back against the tree-trunk. She looked across the field and asked, 'How long have we been walking?'

Julia looked at her watch. 'About twenty minutes. I think this is far enough, don't you? If we have a rest, we'll be able to saunter back and be there long before time.' She looked around. The breeze rustled the leaves in the trees. 'It's a nice spot here. Not a soul in sight!'

Mrs Lawson unscrewed a bottle of water and took a gulp. 'Ah, that's better. I don't do much walking any more. This was long enough for me!'

She took another welcome drink. 'Tell me about yourself Julia. How long have you been doing this job?'

Julia laughed and did.

'So you're not planning on doing it forever then?'

She shook her head. 'No, I'd like to be a teacher. I have a degree, but I need extra qualifications to teach, and that costs money. That's why I took this job.' She drank some water. 'I enjoy it, but I need to think about the future and a permanent, well-paid job.'

'I'm going to have to find a job when we get back,' Susan said. She looked at Julia. 'You know about my divorce?'

Julia nodded. 'Mrs Lawson mentioned it.'

'It's a bit scary to be unemployed. I've been self-employed for fifteen years. Our business was doing well. I've no idea what else I can do.'

Spontaneously Julia said, 'Can't you just carry on?'

Susan looked surprised. 'You mean carry on with the business?'

'Yes, why not?'

'When we separated, we divided everything. The company was closed and we divided the assets. Half a company isn't worth that much.'

'But isn't it possible for you to just start the same kind of business again? If you were successful, it seems silly to look for something else.'

Susan looked thoughtful. 'I've never thought about that.' She paused. 'Theoretically, I could — I suppose. I've my share of our assets and I have a house. I could sell the house and buy a small flat. That would give me more capital. I don't need a house any more. What for?' She looked excited. 'I organised the office and I always kept good contact with our regular customers, most of them were like friends. Yes, I think I could do it again.'

Julia nodded. 'You just need to know if they'll carry on business with you when you're in sole charge. From what I gather, you were the driving force behind the business, so there's a good chance of success. You can always employ someone else to do your ex-husband's job on pay-plus-provision.'

Susan's eyes brightened, and there was colour in her cheeks. She looked a different person. Julia glanced towards Mrs Lawson. She was lying fast asleep with her mouth wide open. Julia and Susan smiled at each other.

Julia leaned back against the rough bark of the tree and left Susan to her own thoughts for a while. She was amused when Susan extracted a note-book from her bag and began to fill the page with notes and figures.

Julia was happy to listen to the wind whispering in the grass and the leaves rattling on the branches of the trees — until it began to sound more threatening. Looking up at the sky, she noticed that the clouds were being whipped across by strong winds, and that the pleasant patches of blues were rapidly being replaced by shades of gloomy greys. She looked at her watch. It was time to leave. She got up, brushed her skirt and touched Mrs Lawson gently. 'Time to go!' Mrs Lawson woke with a start, but smiled at Julia and nodded. She began to fuss around and gather her belongings into her roomy bag.

Susan was already on her feet and shoving her notebook into her shoulder bag. She looked up. 'It doesn't look very promising, does it?'

Julia shook her head. 'No, but we should be all right. If we leave now we'll be back at the bus long before any rain. It looks like there's a storm in the offing.'

They set off. The wind was in their faces, bringing their clothes and their hair into complete disorder. They were soon on the track and feeling happier that they were now within distance of the bus and safety.

By the time they broke through the opening leading down to the beach, they could see everyone crowded round the bus and in the process of boarding. The wind thrashed at the sand, throwing it wickedly at people's arms and legs. On board, Julia stroked her short hair into place, looked around and did a quick mental check that everyone was present. She was about to give Enzo the go ahead to leave when Mrs Lawson gave a small shriek of distress.

'My necklace; I've lost my necklace!'

Julia went to her and looked down at her distressed face. 'Are you sure? Where did you lose it? What does it look like?'

Mrs Lawson was completely downcast. 'Yes, it's gone, I'm sure. It was the last present my husband ever bought me. I wouldn't mind so much if it was any other one, but it was his last gift before he died.' She had tears in her eyes. 'I must have left it by that tree. I was searching through my bag for some sweets and pulled everything out onto the grass.'

Julia noted the first faint murmur of discontent; everyone wanted to get back to the hotel and out of the storm. She decided to act quickly. 'I'll go back and look for it. Everyone is sheltered here in the bus; it shouldn't take too long.'

Mrs Lawson was quick to protest. 'I can't expect you to do that my dear. I'll have to find a way to come back, and go myself to search for it tomorrow if I can.'

Julia answered in a rush of words. 'We're here now. We weren't due to leave for another half-an-hour anyway, so if I hurry we'll still be able to leave roughly on time. It's no bother. Who knows if the necklace will still be there tomorrow? The spot was isolated, but funnier things have happened.' She smiled at the older woman.

Mrs Lawson lifted her hands in protest, but Julia was already on her way. She picked up the microphone from the neighbouring seat to Roark. 'Ladies and Gentlemen, there'll be a short delay until we set off for the hotel, roughly twenty to thirty minutes. Enzo will be coming round to offer you drinks in a few minutes.'

Roark's eyebrows lifted. 'What's going on?'

She explained.

'Don't you think that's a bit fool-hardy? Look outside; it's going to tip down any minute. How can you be sure you'll find this field and that tree?'

She met his glance. 'The necklace means a lot to her. I know exactly where we were. I just need a little time to get there and back. If she said she lost it there, I believe her.'

He shrugged. 'You can't go traipsing off into the countryside on your own. I'd better come with you.'

She was almost too startled to protest, but she did manage. 'That's not necessary. It's enough for one of us to get wet.'

'I know, but I'm not letting you go alone, so the sooner we start, the sooner we'll get back. There are some raincoats in one of our containers.'

'Oh . . . yes, that's right. I'd forgotten. That'll help.'

Julia told Enzo what was going on; he

produced a current DVD film. Once it was running and showing on the various TV screens fixed throughout the coach, he began to circulate with drinks. Reassured, Julia donned the thin transparent raincoat and with Roark at her heels, she went out into the elements.

Struggling along the length of the bus against the increasing wind, she passed Mrs Lawson who gave her a worried look. Julia smiled reassuringly and carried on.

7

As soon as they left the area of the beach, the straggly bordering hedges provided a little protection against the wind, but not much. The plastic raincoat danced about her slim body like a transparent balloon and Julia's skirt was soon soaked. Roark was no better off and Julia had no doubt he was already cursing her for insisting on searching for the necklace.

Holding on to the hood of the raincoat, she looked up at the threatening sky. If anything, it looked more inhospitable than before. She quickened her pace. With Julia in the lead, they reached the gate leading into the field.

Raindrops began to fall, big raindrops, and they were soon wandering through the soaking wet grass towards the tree where Julia and the other two women had sat just a short time ago. The sound of the wind, rain and the approaching thunder and lightning made conversation difficult, so she just pointed to the tree and forged ahead.

When they got there, the branches waving above them provided sparse protection. Julia bent down and began to search the ground where Mrs Lawson had sat. It didn't take long, and she was soon able to hold aloft the missing necklace. Despite the appalling weather, she felt jubilant and beamed at Roark.

Roark viewed her with the rain streaming down her face and couldn't help giving her an answering smile.

She pocketed the necklace. The driving rain increased and flashes of lightning lit the sky accompanied by bouts of intermittent thunder. Roark looked around. On the side of the hill nearby was a small building. He pointed at her, at himself and then at the building.

Julia shook her head and pointed the

way back to the beach. He grabbed her hand and pulled her along behind him. The ground sloped gradually and the surface was slippery; rainwater was streaming down towards them as they climbed. Julia gave in and tried to keep pace with him. She would have slipped a couple of times if Roark hadn't been holding on tight to her hand and wrist.

When they reached the shabby building, they found it was some kind of run-down storage place. There were the remnants of straw and neglected farming implements scattered around, but the roof was intact.

Roark shut the door against the wind and the rain. His hair was soaked and rain trickled from his forehead over his face. He shook the drops free.

Julia threw back the hood and shook her hands too. 'Phew! What a downpour. I don't think I've ever been out in anything like it.'

'Nor me, but I don't think it's very unusual in this particular area. When it rains, it really rains. There's no point in trying to fight our way back. We'll wait here until things have calmed down.'

'What about the bus? They'll worry if we don't turn up on time. Someone else might come looking.'

He took off his plastic raincoat and threw it over a nearby bale. Fishing in his breast pocket, he pulled out his phone and a visiting card. 'I have Enzo's number, just in case. I think it'll be best for him to take everyone back to the hotel as soon as it's safe to drive. When we get out of here, we'll find a taxi to take us home.'

Julia's eyes widened. 'Is that necessary? It'll be over soon.'

He shook his head. 'I don't think so.' He went to the small window and looked out. 'It's almost pitch dark out there and we are right in the middle of the storm. It might be quite a while until we can walk back, and even then it won't be very pleasant.'

Julia joined him, looked out, and was forced to agree. 'Okay, go ahead. Oh! Tell Enzo to reassure Mrs Lawson that her necklace is safe.'

Grumbling under his breath about the damned necklace, he punched in the number and spoke with Enzo. Julia listened as he explained the situation. 'Use your own judgement. Leave when you think it's safe but don't take any chances. We may not be able to get back for a while. Don't worry about us, take the people to the hotel as soon as possible; we'll find our own way back.'

Julia was glad she was wearing her blazer. It wasn't very warm and her skirt was soaking. There wasn't any prospect of making a fire either. Roark didn't smoke, and neither did she, so there wasn't much likelihood that someone had a lighter in their pocket.

He put the phone back in his jacket and dragged some of the bales of hay out of the corner. Covering them with their raincoats, dry sides up, he made a sweeping gesture. 'We may as well sit while we wait.'

Making herself comfortable, and with her arms gripping the side of the bale, she said, 'It was good of you to come; just think, you could be sitting in the bus, watching James Bond and drinking hot coffee.'

He smiled benignly. 'Don't remind me.'

The knowledge that she was alone with him in this gloomy hut, miles from anywhere made her senses spin and she told herself not to be silly.

'I'm sure Mrs Lawson will be very grateful to us. That's a big consolation, isn't it?'

His honesty won the day. 'Not much.'

Julia laughed. 'Well, I'm glad we came. As far as I understand it, the necklace was one of her husband's last gifts so this is not just because of its material worth — it's the memories that are important. I think Mrs Lawson is very well off, she could afford to lose a necklace and not care.'

'Where is it?'

Julia fumbled in the pocket of the raincoat and handed him the gold and sapphire necklace. Roark whistled. 'I bet it's worth a pretty penny. Anyone would be sorry to lose this. Those sapphires really gleam, even in this shadowy light.'

Julia watched him handling it and her gaze riveted on his long artistic fingers. She reminded herself that they had both been so let down in the past. He'd stated quite firmly that he'd never be caught up in marriage again, and Mike had robbed her of any illusions about love.

Perhaps one day, someday, she'd learn to trust again and, if she was lucky, she might fall in love with someone who loved her. She definitely didn't intend to let any man come between her and her aim to achieve independency. Mike had used her to set his own feet on the ladder to success. She was determined that no man would ever use her, and then discard her, like that again.

Roark Ellis was a damaged character too; he'd put up the shutters to protect himself from any meaningful future relationship. In all probability, he was red-blooded enough to be satisfied with an occasional affair to fulfil his needs, but he wouldn't go beyond that — he'd said so. It wasn't enough for her to be attracted to someone who wasn't looking for a love of a lifetime; someone who just wanted an affair. Julia coloured at her own thoughts. She wasn't interested in him, was she?

His deep voice interrupted her thoughts. 'You mentioned that you had a bad experience with your boyfriend? That it had all collapsed overnight. What happened? You don't have to tell me, of course, if you think I'm being too inquisitive.'

'No, I don't mind. There's nothing unusual about it. He used me to get his MA — I worked so that he could study. Then he found himself a new girlfriend and when I finally grasped what was going on, I packed my bags and left.'

Roark ran a hand through his hair. 'Still bitter?'

She stretched her legs out in a straight line. 'I don't know if bitter is the right description. I was mad, disillusioned, and very hurt at the time. Now I'm still mad, but with myself for being such a dupe. I can't even remember what attracted me to him in the first place. My common sense should have told me someone who was prepared to let someone else work for them, while they achieved their own aims wasn't much of a catch. My parents and Gran warned me, but you know what it's like, there's a rebellious streak in all of us . . . I thought I knew better.'

He was facing her and he leaned forward; his hand came down over hers possessively. 'He was a very stupid man. I'm quite sure that he'll soon regret that he didn't hang on to you.'

Julia had the wildest urge to jump back from the effect his hand was having on her. She was saved from further confusion when he withdrew it and gave her a smile instead. Shakily she replied, 'I don't think so. He already had a replacement, and he had his MA in his pocket. When I left, he was busy with interviews and thought his life was taking off at last.'

'But he did it at your expense. One day it will catch up with him. He'll realise he threw away the best thing anyone can have — loyalty and love.'

There was inherent strength in his face and his eyes were a compelling grey. Julia also discovered that he could smile unexpectedly with good humour and it made her feel better. She nodded wordlessly. He got up and strode to the grimy window, and then swivelled slowly to face her again.

'I think it's easing off a little. It's a pity we can't make a fire; that would cheer us up no end.'

Julia was glad of normality. 'I thought about that too, but we don't have a lighter, do we?'

He shook his head. 'I've got some chewing gum.'

Julia laughed. 'Not much use, I'm

afraid. How long will this weather last, do you think?'

He shrugged. 'Hard to say.' He came back and made himself comfortable on their makeshift seat.

Julia was always impressed with his commanding air of self-confidence. She hesitated, but reasoned she'd bared her soul to him, so why shouldn't she ask questions. 'And your experiences with your ex-wife? Has it made you bitter?'

He dug his hands deep into his pockets. 'Probably. I try not to think about it much any more. After the legal bickering was over, I was glad to change my surroundings and make a new start. It was good to be able to direct my energy into my work. I'd never had any really disturbing experiences until my wife blew the top off everything.' His expression was clouded; his eyes were reproachful. 'You live and learn.'

She nodded. 'Sobering, but it's not fatal, is it?'

His mouth twisted wryly and he gave her a weak smile. 'It's strange; I can talk to you about it, but I don't think I have very much with anyone else since it happened. Even the family avoids the subject. They probably think it's too upsetting. It was, but I'm adjusting slowly.'

'Perhaps it's because there's a kind of parallel between us. Even if our boats were different sizes, we both got sunk, didn't we?'

He laughed. 'True.'

'I'm not going to let Mike spoil my life. I'm going to concentrate on something worthwhile. You ought to do the same.'

'I try. It's hard to forget. Someone like me, who's been used to more success than failure, finds it hard to accept.'

'Put it down to experience. It wasn't your failure. As far as I can tell, you did your best to make your relationship work, just like I did with Mike.'

'I hope so.'

Julia got up and went to the window. There were the first couple of weak rays of sunshine breaking through the dark clouds. 'It looks like the sky's clearing at last.'

He joined her. His answering smile brought an immediate softening to his features. 'You're right. Let's get our jackets and go.' He looked at his watch. 'Enzo probably took off with the first ray of sunshine. I expect we'll have to walk to the nearest village and order a taxi.'

The prospect didn't bother her. When they were leaving, she looked back over her shoulder at the abandoned bales of hay among the dancing shadows. 'It was a perfect spot to weather the storm. If we'd had a fire, I'd be reluctant to leave.'

A smile ruffled Roark's mouth. 'I'll remember to carry a tab of matches at all times in future.'

He walked ahead of her and hesitated in his tracks for a second to look at the surroundings, so that Julia collided with him. They were so close that when she looked up her heart hammered in her ears and his eyes riveted her to the spot. The ensuing touch of his lips was a delicious sensation and she felt a shock run through her. They both froze. Julia noticed the complete surprise on his face and then a definite hardening of his eyes. His voice was curt when he said, 'Sorry! I shouldn't have done that.'

To her annoyance, she found herself starting to blush. 'It's okay, Roark.' She tried to find some suitable words to reassure him, and couldn't find any fast enough.

He turned suddenly on his heel and stormed off down the incline towards the fields and the track beyond. Julia couldn't see his face, but she could tell from the energy he was expending that he was irritated. She hesitated for a second, torn by conflicting emotions then she set out after him. Julia didn't understand why he was so mad. He must know she was adult enough not to set any store by their kiss. They'd both admitted to each other that they were trying to avoid emotional traps. He'd given in to a spur of the moment sentimentality, friendship, sympathy, perhaps sheer kindness.

On their way back to the coast, she followed a silent, hurrying figure. By the time they reached the beach, the wind was reduced to a moderate gentleness although it was still blowing his hair into an untidy shape when she finally faced him. Mixed feeling surged through her but she tried to sound offhand. 'Is it far to the next village? Any idea which direction?'

He seemed almost relieved to follow her lead. 'It's roughly half a mile, in that direction.' He pointed.

She was swimming through a haze of new feelings about him. 'Let's go. The sooner we get there, the sooner we'll be back at the hotel. If we don't turn up for dinner on time, they'll probably call the police.'

Without any more ado, they set off in the direction he'd indicated. While she was marching along, she wondered what had happened to her resolve not to think twice about any man again until she knew he was the right one for her. Roark Ellis wasn't the right man for her or any other woman. He was so rooted in his past, no one from the present stood a chance.

They found a taxi number pasted to a wall near the lone telephone box, but it still took a time for the driver to find them. He came from the neighbouring town and passengers weren't usually waiting to be picked up on a nameless street in an isolated little village.

* * *

They got back to the hotel in time for a shower before dinner. Julia restored the necklace to Mrs Lawson and she was rewarded by hugs and effusive thanks. She joined her and Susan and tried to ignore Roark sitting at one of the other tables.

The evening meal was pleasant, everyone seemed very relaxed and the main topic of conversation was the storm and its outcome. Roark stared steadily at his table companions.

Julia was almost glad to escape to her room and have an early night. She started to read her paperback but when she realised she'd been reading the same paragraph over-and-over again for the last five minutes, she threw it angrily in the corner and put out the light to escape from silly thoughts about whether she was responsible for his behaviour. She knew that she wasn't.

★   ★   ★

Next morning, she was up early, and had finished having breakfast before most of the other guests arrived. She went to sit out on the narrow terrace in front of the hotel. Roark joined her. He stood in front of her looking more than a little uncomfortable.

'Julia, I . . . I hope you didn't get the wrong impression . . . about my kissing you yesterday?'

She reacted angrily and her temper flared. She'd been mulling it over for too long to pooh-pooh it now. 'No, I didn't, I know where you stand, so don't give it another thought. I fail to understand why you're making a big thing out of it unless of course you're scared to admit you can still feel something for a woman, any woman, after all.'

'Don't be so childish!' The angry retort hardened his features.

'I'm not being childish, you are. You are also being insensitive because you're determined to warn me how futile it'd be for me to get any wrong idea about you. You're warning me off, but I assure you that's not necessary. I'm not a scatter-brained teenager, and I'm not easily impressed any more. It was only a kiss, and it wasn't even a proper one either!' she finished angrily.

There was a suggestion of annoyance in his eyes, and she was glad.

She got up and moved away quickly. She turned suddenly and said, 'Let's keep everything strictly professional from now on, okay? You don't need to sit near me in the bus, or in the restaurant any more — then you can relax and enjoy your own company. The tour finishes tomorrow, and then you'll never see me again.'

Her mouth had a resolute look as she moved towards the hotel entrance with long purposeful strides. Why did she ever think he was someone worth knowing? He was someone worth avoiding.

The rest of the tour went off smoothly. It was easier than Julia imagined. She and Roark treated each other like acquaintances whenever their paths crossed. If any of the tour members noticed, no one mentioned it to Julia. Each of them concentrated on their own work and did their best to keep the tour participants happy. They went their own ways in their leisure time. If Roark felt any regrets that their tentative friendship had been torpe-doed, he gave no indication. Julia tried not to agonise over the situation and masked her inner uncertainty with deceptive calm.

✷ ✷ ✷

Back at Gatwick, they stood side by side and said goodbye to everyone. Mrs Lawson waited until last and had a bundle of money in her hand.

She held it in Julia's direction. 'I want you to have an extra something, so that you know how grateful I am that you found my necklace. It was extremely kind and thoughtful to help me in such appalling weather.'

Julia was flustered and embarrassed. She cupped Mrs Lawson's hands in hers, around the money. 'It's very kind Mrs Lawson, but the company has strict rules about us not accepting any kind of tips. Even if they didn't, I wouldn't want to take any kind of reward from you. I was glad we found it and brought it back despite the weather. I know it means a lot to you, and Mr Ellis and I were glad to help.'

Roark was standing next to her and nodded.

Mrs Lawson looked unhappy. 'But it's only a fraction of what the necklace is worth.'

Julia smiled. 'Perhaps, but I won't accept it. I hope you have a good journey home, and that we'll see you on another trip with Likely Prospects sometime in the not too distant future.'

The older woman shrugged. 'I'll remember you, and the company. I had a lovely time.'

'Good. That's what the company wants to hear.'

Mrs Lawson reached forward and hugged Julia briefly before she said, 'Bye — till next time.'

Mrs Lawson began to pull her suitcase along towards the exit to the taxi ranks. When she was almost out of sight, Julia held out her hand to him.

'Bye Roark. It was nice to meet you on another tour. I think it went well, don't you? I don't suppose we'll meet again. All the best.'

He took her hand and held it for a fraction too long. 'Yes, I think so too. Everyone seemed very satisfied, even the demanding ones. I wish you luck with your course when you start, and hope you find a good job afterwards.'

She nodded, took hold of her suitcase handle and turned away. It didn't occur to him to suggest they travel into London together, or perhaps he had thought about it but dismissed the idea. She straightened her shoulders — who needed him anyway?

8

Five days later, she started out on another tour; this time it was Burgundy. It was interesting because she'd never been there and the medieval churches and abbeys were cradled in wooded landscapes that were a delight to the eye and the senses. The tour lecturer was a specialist in medieval architecture who knew her job and handled the group extremely well. It should have been pleasure all the way, but Julia was annoyed when she unconsciously found herself looking around for a tall figure with thin features and an air of solitude.

★   ★   ★

They were now on the run-up to Christmas and Julia couldn't quite believe the weeks had passed so quickly.

Delivering the Burgundy documentation to head office, her heart missed a beat when she saw Roark coming towards her. He had two women with him and his arm was round one of them. Somewhat disconcerted, she continued onwards. She couldn't pretend she hadn't seen them and go the other way. Her heart was beating fast and her breath caught in her lungs as Roark came closer. He looked well and there was even a sparkle in his eyes. His hand dropped from the woman's shoulder as they came face-to-face.

'Hello, Julia. What a nice surprise. What are you doing here?'

His strong features held her spellbound again for a few seconds and then she dragged her attention to the two women with him. His voice set her insides tingling. She hadn't seen him since they'd parted at the airport after Basilicata, but with blinding certainty she suddenly knew that she'd fallen in love with him.

He was an introverted, complicated

character, but he was so special. He was his own man who made his own decisions and went his own way. She admired his intellect, but he also sent her senses spinning in a very non-intellectual way. With a lump the size of a mountain in her throat, she managed to reply sensibly. 'Hello Roark. I'm just finding out where my next tour goes.'

He smiled and his eyes sparkled. 'Any idea?'

'Germany, for six days I think, and then Paris just before Christmas.'

'Lovely places; wrong time of year.'

It was as if they'd never been irritated with each other. 'Perhaps, but everyone says Berlin is an exciting place no matter what season it is. If I'm lucky I'll be able to do some Christmas shopping.'

He nodded and suddenly remembered his companions. 'Oh . . . this is Fiona, and my sister Lynne.'

A dark haired, pert, pretty and smartly dressed woman held out her hand. 'Hello. Pleased to meet you. I've heard all about you already.'

Julia shook hands and nodded.

The second woman resembled Roark, and Julia smiled in her direction. 'Hello, nice to meet you.'

Her smile was returned. 'Hello.'

'We've been to remind Keith to join us for lunch; it's my sister's birthday,' Roark explained, then he hesitated. 'Would you like to join us?'

The temptation was great; she longed to say yes, but her path and Roark's were not likely to cross again, once she left Likely Prospects, so she may as well start to accept that now. She tried to store how he looked in her memory, but it wasn't really necessary. His face was already firmly entrenched there, and had been for weeks. She tried to hold his glance. 'That's very kind, but I have a lunch date too, after I've seen Joel.' She singled his sister out. 'Happy Birthday! I hope you have an enjoyable time.'

'Thanks!'

His sister had the same grey eyes.

Julia wanted to get away. 'I won't keep you, and I have to run myself — or I'll be late. It was nice to meet you both. Bye Roark!' Without waiting for his reaction, she sidled past his sister and went inside. She didn't see the slight look of regret on his face, or how the two women exchanged knowing looks.

Joel was her contact person in the company these days, and she took the paperwork along to the office and chatted to him for a while.

'You've almost finished your contract, haven't you?'

'Yes.'

'Are you going to extend?'

Julia was silent for a second.

'Don't worry; this is just between you and me. I know that you have other plans. I only ask because Keith mentioned that he'd need to have a talk with you soon. I thought I should warn you.'

'I was expecting that. I won't take another contract if I'm offered one. I've almost saved enough money to get me through a course I want to take. Perhaps I'll have to find a weekend job as well to fill out my funds.'

He nodded understandingly. 'I haven't quite worked out your next tours. Can you give me a call after the weekend?'

'Of course. I'll really miss being a part of Likely Prospects. I've seen some super places that I'd never have seen otherwise, and I've learned a lot.'

Joel viewed her kindly. 'When you're a fully-paid working woman, you'll have enough money to go on one of our tours as a guest.'

She laughed softly. 'Not likely, not for a long, long time. I've plenty of other things to do with my money once I'm in a paid job.' She shouldered her bag. 'I'll be off; I'll call in on Monday. I'm coming into town to do some Christmas shopping.'

'Yes, okay.' She was on her way to the door, when Joel said, 'Oh, almost forgot, this envelope came the other day, addressed to you.' He handed her a fat, buff envelope, with her name and the company's address on it. She didn't recognise the handwritting, but she took it and lifted her hand in farewell.

Julia wandered down the corridor to the lift. Waiting for it to arrive, she slit the envelope and found it contained a fistful of bank notes and a short letter. Surprised, she read the note quickly. It was from Mrs Lawson, who was again trying to be generous. It was tempting, but Julia knew she couldn't accept it. The lift opened and she came face-to-face with Claudia.

Taken aback, Julia coloured slightly. She didn't know what to say. She managed. 'Hello Claudia.'

If Claudia felt uncomfortable, it didn't show. 'Hi! Still touring?'

'Yes. How . . . how are you?'

'Fine. I'm starting with a similar set-up in a couple of weeks' time. I'm here to pick up the rest of my insurance records, papers and things.'

Julia nodded and tried to show sympathy. 'Good. It's never enjoyable to be out of work, is it?'

Claudia shrugged and stroked her perfectly arranged hair. 'Actually I wouldn't mind being out of work if I had enough money to afford to be a lady of leisure, or had someone to support me. It's much more comfortable than being part of the rat-race all the time.' Her pale eyebrows lifted as she pointedly studied the bundle of notes in Julia's hand.

Julia answered Claudia without being asked. 'One of the people on the last tour but-one sent me this. She wanted to give me some money when the tour ended because I did her a special favour on the trip. I tried to tell her we don't accept tips; it seems though she won't take no for an answer. I'll have to send it back to her, when I find out exactly where she lives.'

Claudia laughed. 'Most people wouldn't think twice about keeping it. Who's to know?' She looked at her watch. 'Must go. Keith is a stickler for punctuality.' She adjusted her shoulder bag. 'I just saw Roark outside; going down the street in the opposite direction. How is he?'

'Did you?' The colour shot into her face. She didn't want to talk to Claudia about Roark. 'As far as I know he's fine.' Julia's colour was high. 'Ask Keith.'

Claudia smirked and gave Julia a derisory look. 'I honestly didn't think you'd make it with him. Believe me, Roark wants someone top class and you don't have that kind of status. I heard that his ex-wife is back again. Perhaps she's hoping to return to the nest again, and he's willing to welcome her.'

Julia felt a sense of loss and wondered if she'd just seen Roark outside, with his wife. She couldn't stop herself asking. 'How do you know?'

'I'm friendly with Keith's secretary. I get my information from her. It always pays to know the right people.'

'It's devious to choose friends and acquaintances based on whether they'll be useful to you.'

Claudia laughed. 'Think so? We all have our own methods to get through life. Cheerio!'

Julia's throat tightened and her fists clenched tightly as Claudia turned away. She was still the malicious person she'd always been. Julia stepped into the lift and saw Claudia walking down the corridor until the doors cut off her view.

★ ★ ★

Once home, she found Mrs Lawson's address easily via the internet, packed the money in a new bubble envelope and sent it back by registered post with a brief letter of explanation.

After a relaxing weekend with Gran and meeting someone she knew from her university days, Julia looked forward to a morning of shopping in London. She didn't intend to spend much but she needed a new pair of boots and it was time to look tentatively around for some Christmas presents. She decided to go to the office first.

Joel was behind his desk and looked

153

up when she came in. He ruffled the papers and managed a weak smile. 'Hi! Keith wants to see you straight away when you come in, so I suggest you go there and call back for details of the next tour?'

Keith probably wanted to find out about a second contract. Joel couldn't plan her into the arrangements beyond Christmas unless he knew one way or the other. She nodded. 'Okay. Be back soon; I don't suppose our chat will take too long.'

She went to Keith's office. His secretary looked up. 'Morning Julia.' She buzzed her boss and Keith came out and motioned her to precede him into his office.

'Make yourself comfortable. I expect you know why I wanted to see you this morning?'

Settling in her chair, she said, 'I presume it's about my contract?'

'Yes, that and something else that's cropped up and needs clearing.'

She was puzzled. 'What?'

'Someone told me you were accepting tips from one of our guests.'

The breath left her lungs and her voice pitched higher. 'I did what!'

'That you were given a cash tip recently from someone who'd been on one of our tours. Is it true?'

She swallowed hard, trying not to reveal her anger. 'Yes. Mrs Lawson sent me some money; she was one of the tour members to Basilicata. She sent it here to the office and Joel gave me the envelope last Friday. I presume it was Claudia who told you that she saw me with the money?'

'Yes, it was.'

'I didn't keep it.'

'Can you prove that?'

Her face paled. She tried to think logically. Julia rummaged in her bag and triumphantly emerged with the proof of the registered letter to Mrs Lawson. She handed it to him. 'I sent it back, registered, first thing on Saturday morning.'

There was a look of relief in his eyes.

'I didn't believe you'd break company rules. I hope you'll understand when I say we'll need to confirm Mrs Lawson has received the money. This slip doesn't say what was enclosed in the envelope.'

Swallowing, she got up. 'Please do. Her address must be in your records, but I got it from the telephone directory online.' Still feeling a little dazed, she added, 'Now that I'm here anyway, I may as well tell you I won't be extending my contract.'

He looked flustered. 'I hope your decision has nothing to do with this business? Claudia does seem to have had it in for you, from the very beginning, and I never understood why. You presented no danger to her; your jobs were in completely different areas of the business. She was permanent and you were on contract. Do you know why?'

Julia licked her lips and the picture of Roark zipped through her brain. She had no doubt what the reason was.

'No . . . Claudia and I were never the best of friends, but some people just never hit it off, do they? I expect there are fewer tours on offer at this time of year so if you want me to leave before the official date, just say so.'

He lifted his hand. 'You are planned in until just before Christmas. I hope you know I wasn't accusing you just now. I just want to be able to stuff Claudia's words down her throat if she starts any trouble. We emphasise in all our brochures that everything is inclusive and that tips or backhanders are not accepted. It would be very bad publicity if someone suggested anything else.'

Julia relaxed slightly. 'It's okay. There's no harm done. I'm sure Mrs Lawson will confirm I returned the money. She tried to give me money once before, when the tour ended, and I refused her then too — Roark will confirm that. Mrs Lawson is causing complications, isn't she?'

He nodded. 'Please, think seriously

again about extending the contract. I'd like you to stay; people have always been extremely happy in your care.'

Julia gave him a wavering smile. 'I'm not leaving because I don't like it here. I needed to earn money so that I can get extra qualifications to be able to teach, and I'm able to do that now.' She held out her hand.

Keith looked uneasy as he shook it. 'Joel has already planned you in for Berlin next week and Paris just before Christmas. I'll be sorry to see you go.'

Julia nodded. 'If we don't meet again, I'd like to say thanks for everything. You have my present address, if any more questions crop up?'

'Yes.'

'I'll be on my way then. Bye.'

'Bye.'

Outside Keith's office and in the corridor again, she breathed deeply.

She left the office building and tightened her scarf as she met the impact of the wintery winds. The trees were now bare skeletons and the whole scene was very bleak in comparison to the leafy ripeness of how it had looked when she first started with Likely Prospects.

9

She got the rough schedule for her next tour from Joel. It wasn't exactly a wonderful season to visit Germany, but they were visiting Dresden, Potsdam and Berlin. The weather was still mild, even if they'd probably need warm coats all the time.

The flight from Heathrow to Dresden was direct. After a city tour and a visit to a museum, they were now on their second day, and about to leave to visit the Green Vault of the Residenzschloss, when Julia was called to the telephone. It was Joel.

'Sorry to be the bringer of bad news. Your gran has been taken to hospital. A neighbour found her lying in the hall early this morning; she was unconscious, and still is. This neighbour knew that you worked for Likely Prospects and got in touch with us. The hospital wants to see a relation as soon as possible.'

Julia's knees felt wobbly. 'How serious is it?'

'I don't know, but if the hospital is looking for a relative, it's not a good sign, is it?'

Her mind was buzzing. 'No.' She was silent for a moment. 'I'm in the middle of this tour. How can I get away?'

'Don't worry, Lisa is already en route. She'll be coming out on the next available flight. You pack your bags and wait at the hotel for her. The lecturer will have to double up and handle your part of the tour this morning. Once Lisa arrives, hot-foot it back to London. You should be here sometime this afternoon. Lisa will bring you an open ticket to use for a flight back. If you let us know your time of arrival, we'll arrange a pick-up.'

'Thanks Joel, I appreciate it.'

'Don't thank me, thank Keith. He set the ball rolling as soon as he heard. He's a taxing old so-and-so sometimes, but he comes out on top when it really matters.'

'Which hospital?'

He told her, and then said, 'Pass the phone to the lecturer — it's Tom Bristol, isn't it? I'll explain the situation to him. My advice to you is to drink a small cognac, settle your nerves if you can, and then start packing.'

Her brain still in a whirl, she murmured, 'Thanks. Hang on, I'll get Tom, he's outside with the group waiting for the bus to arrive.'

★ ★ ★

From then on, Julia's thoughts circled around Gran. She didn't know whether to inform her parents before she'd spoken to the doctors at the hospital. In the end she decided to wait.

As soon as her replacement arrived, she set off for the airport and took the first possible flight to London. It was late afternoon when she disembarked in Heathrow. Leaving arrivals, she looked around and was dazed to see Roark waiting.

He held out his hand for her trolley-bag.

Her voice was too sharp. 'What are you doing here?'

'Keith phoned and told me what had happened. As we'd been on two tours together, I thought you'd appreciate someone you knew who'd help to get you to the hospital. Are you okay? It's a bit of a shock I expect, I know you're close to your gran.'

She nodded. She was already mixed up because of Gran's accident; Roark's unexpected appearance confused her even more.

He tucked his hand under her elbow and gently led her towards the exit doors. 'My car's just outside. You'll want to go straight to the hospital? Which one is it?'

She told him and he nodded.

She pulled herself together. 'Look Roark, this is extremely kind, but I'll be alright on my own. You don't have to feel responsible. I'll get a taxi.'

'I'd like to help. It's no trouble. My car is this way.'

When they reached the hospital, he was lucky to find a place to park in a nearby street. She didn't stop him when he got out and went with her towards the entrance. She let him find out where her gran was being treated, and he took her to the nearest lift. Julia gave up trying to dissuade him; he'd clearly made up his mind to help whether she wanted him to, or not. After a quick explanation to the sister in charge, she was allowed to see her gran in intensive care.

Gran looked frail in the hospital gown. Tears rushed to Julia's eyes as she gently stroked the lined forehead and waxy cheeks. Gran's eyelids were closed and she was surrounded by machines. She seemed to be sleeping peacefully. All kinds of memories shot through Julia's brain. Gran was an integral part of her life; she'd always been Julia's haven in a storm. Time slipped by as she stroked Gran's hands, attached to tubes and measuring devices. Glancing at the silent figure in the bed, she quietly left the room and went to where she'd left Roark — he was still sitting in the corridor.

Wiping the remains of tears away with the back of her hand before she reached him, she tried to give him a weak smile. 'Still here?' She sighed. 'She looks so fragile with all that machinery around her, and she's so silent — not my gran at all! I'm going to see if I can find a doctor who knows what's going on, so that I can phone my parents.'

He got up. 'I thought you might want to do that. I asked the sister to find out if there was someone on duty who can give you some detailed information. She'll come for you as soon as a doctor is free. Like a coffee? There's a machine just down the corridor.'

'Please!'

He quickly returned with a cup of hot liquid. Julia had tasted better coffee but it did her good and it helped steady her nerves. A doctor came eventually and they went with him to the sister's office. Julia asked Roark to come with her; it suddenly seemed sensible to have someone around.

The doctor looked at some charts. 'Your grandmother is doing well.' Julia sighed with relief. 'But she isn't quite out of the woods yet. We don't know how long she'll remain unconscious. We don't know what happened, although we presume she fell down stairs. There aren't many bodily injuries apart from some bruising and a broken bone in one hand, so we think she may have only fallen the last couple of steps before she hit her head on something. Luckily, her neighbour must have found her soon after she fell. She's stable and it's now a case of waiting until things improve.'

Julia felt a little better. 'So she isn't in any immediate danger then?'

'No. The only serious possibility is there could be some kind of brain damage. She hasn't fractured her skull, but the brain is the centre of the nervous system and it regulates all kinds of bodily processes. I'll be a lot happier when she regains consciousness.' He looked at her drawn and tired face. 'Take my advice and get some sleep. You could wait around here for hours, days, even weeks before something happens. Leave your details with the sister, and come back again tomorrow.'

Julia nodded like an automaton.

She went back to visit Gran while Roark went to give the sister Julia's address and telephone number. Julia then followed Roark to his car.

Once they were settled, he said, 'It doesn't sound too bad. I'm sure that if they'd suspected massive brain damage in some way, he would have tried to prepare you.'

Julia stared into the murky darkness ahead and nodded.

He started the engine and drove off. A few minutes later, Julia registered they were in a strange part of London.

'We're going in the wrong direction.'

Out of the darkness, he replied, 'I thought it would be a good idea for you to come back with me. I've given them my telephone number for tonight. I've a comfortable couch, and I'll make us something to eat. I'm closer to the hospital than your gran's house.'

Her eyes widened. 'You can't take my problems onto your shoulders Roark. I'm grateful, of course, but this is my dilemma, not yours. I'll be alright at Gran's and I can get a taxi to the hospital.'

'I'd like to help, and my place is only minutes away from the hospital.'

Julia was pulled in two directions. She let her heart decide and remained silent as he drove on.

He pulled into a cul-de-sac and opened the garage door with an automatic control. Driving inside the door closed behind them and he got out. Julia followed. Lifting her bag out of the boot, he motioned towards a door at the side. 'The flat is compact, but it's all I need at the moment.'

'And you're sure I won't be in the way?'

He shook his head and surveyed her kindly. 'No, of course not.'

The tiny hall led into a large living-cum-dining room with a built-in kitchen separated from the rest of the room by a breakfast bar. The walls were covered in full-length bookshelves, jam-packed with all kinds of literature. There was a large leather couch and a couple of roomy armchairs huddled around a Victorian fireplace. A table lamp on a low chest of drawers in front of the window threw gentle light onto the Persian carpet. The room was cosy and welcoming. Julia guessed he'd chosen everything himself. There were no flowers, no green plants, no colourful cushions, and not many decorative touches. It was a man's world.

Roark came in behind her and stood her trolley to one side. 'The bathroom and the bedroom are upstairs. I'll just see what I have in the fridge. Why don't you phone your parents and put them in the picture?'

A couple of minutes later, Julia left her father absorbing the news, and already planning their journey for first thing the next morning.

As if it was perfectly natural to have her around, Roark had left her to explore; he was already bustling around in the kitchen. She went to help.

Even though she had one ear concentrated on the telephone, deep down Julia was storing the memories. He expertly grilled steaks while Julia made a salad from cucumber and lettuce. Julia found she was hungry; perhaps it was because she was sharing a meal with him.

After they finished, he insisted on clearing up and loading the dishwasher. She wandered over to the bookshelves examining and exploring. 'Gosh, you have loads of wonderful books. Some of them are pretty rare, aren't they?'

He smiled and his eyes twinkled; Julia's pulse accelerated.

'Yes, I've spent a lot of time searching for some of them. Many are presents from friends or family — everyone knows how much I like books. I'm going to have to get rid of some of them, or move to a bigger flat soon!'

They sat opposite each other later chatting about things over a glass of red wine; it felt so right. As much as she loved being with Roark, her eyes darted to the phone now and then.

He could tell she was concerned. 'You can't do anything; you know that, don't you?'

She nodded. 'I know, but it doesn't stop me worrying.'

They listened to music, talked about films they'd both seen, and bits and pieces about their families. She felt comfortable and at home with him, and she could tell he felt so too. Eventually, they both agreed it was late, and even though Julia knew she wouldn't be able to sleep, she didn't want to keep Roark up. A brief visit to the bathroom, and she was ready. She was rustling through her bag looking for suitable nightwear, when he came back with an armful of blankets and pillows.

'I think you'll find the couch is quite comfortable. My sister uses it very often and she's never complained. It's wide enough for you to toss and turn.' His dark eyes never left her for an instant. 'Goodnight!'

'Goodnight, and thank you again, for everything.'

'Don't mention it. I'm glad I was around.' He left, closing the door quietly.

As expected, she couldn't sleep. She thought about Gran, and about Roark. As he'd suggested, she did toss and turn and the tidy bed was soon a muddle of blankets wrapped round her body. Eventually she got up and drank some water. She gave up trying to sleep.

Soon after Roark knocked softly on the door and came in. He was barefoot, in cotton boxer shorts, and the muscles rippled under the simple white T-shirt. He moved with easy grace and ran his fingers through his thick dark hair as he neared her. There was a trace of stubble on his chin.

'I heard you moving about. Can't sleep, eh?' he said, sympathetically.

She felt guilty. 'Did I disturb you? Sorry! I'm all right. Go back to bed.' Julia was acutely conscious of his tall athletic physique.

He looked at his watch. 'It'll be daylight soon. Perhaps you'll feel better waiting at the hospital until your parents turn up? I'll get dressed and take you there.'

'I can get a taxi.'

He didn't wait to reply. 'Back in five minutes.'

She changed into jeans, boots and a warm top, and was ready to go when he returned.

★ ★ ★

This time there was little to be seen or heard of the city's bustle and hum. It had rained in the night and the surface mirrored the lamplights as they drove along. She was silent for a few minutes.

He commented on the empty road and Julia could tell he was trying to think of something to divert her thoughts in other directions. Changing the subject, he asked, 'What exactly happened when your boyfriend tricked you? How did you find out?'

'He used me, I told you that when we talked about it before.'

When she looked at his shadowy profile, she saw him nod. She didn't really understand why he wanted to know, but waiting for a traffic light to change, Julia began to explain in detail and finished the story a few minutes later. She felt stupid when she heard her own explanation.

His retort was sharp and instant. 'How could you let him take advantage of you like that? You must have realised that someone who was prepared to let you bear the financial burden while he steamed ahead wasn't worth the air he breathed.'

Julia was already mad with herself, and his remark didn't improve her mood. 'I wasn't more stupid than you were. It's the pot calling the kettle black, isn't it? You were blind enough to let your wife have numerous affairs behind your back.' Julia could have bit her tongue, but it was too late. There was a heavy silence between them. Julia was relieved when he manoeuvred the car into a spot next to the entrance door.

If she'd had more time, she might have tried to smooth things over, but as it was, she just hurried to get out. 'Stay where you are, I'll get my bag. Thanks for bringing me. Don't wait around. I'm all right now.' He didn't answer. 'I'm honestly grateful for everything you've done for me.' She closed the boot with a bang and hurried towards the entrance doors without another look back.

10

To everyone's relief Gran regained consciousness two days later and there was no lasting damage. She complained that her little finger in plaster would prevent her sticking it out when she drank her tea 'like a lady', but Julia could tell she was as relieved as everyone else was.

After various tests had been made and the doctor gave his approval, she was allowed to go home. Julia's parents stayed a few days, but as Gran refused to go home with them, they set off for Chester comforting themselves with the thought that she would be coming with Julia for Christmas and had agreed to stay longer with them than she'd originally promised to do.

A neighbour assured them she would keep an eye on Gran when Julia was away on the last tour of her contract.

Julia didn't try to contact Roark. She remembered her bad-tempered outburst in the car park of the hospital; he must believe she was a silly, immature woman.

*   *   *

Julia came back from getting some shopping for Gran, keen to stock up before she had to leave for her next trip overseas. Gran handed her a visiting card. Julia glanced at it and her eyes widened in surprise. 'Mike? Where did this come from?'

'He called after you left, in a flashy car, and brought those.' Gran nodded to a couple of cardboard boxes sitting in the corner. 'He said they were your things . . . and also told me to tell you he hopes you'll get in touch soon.' She absentmindedly polished the surface of the banister while watching her granddaughter's face.

Julia looked at the card for a moment before she tore it into tiny pieces. She realised how little Mike had ever meant to her.

Gran beamed and held out her hand for the bits. 'Good girl! I'll dispose of that rubbish with great pleasure.'

That same evening when they were watching TV, Gran surprised her completely when she told Julia that Roark had visited her in hospital. Apparently, he'd brought her some fruit, explained who he was, and how he was involved. Gran stated he was a 'very nice young man, with excellent manners, a good sense of humour, and someone she liked from the word go.' Julia wondered what they'd talked about and why Gran didn't find it strange that an unfamiliar man had visited her in hospital. She decided not to ask because Gran might ask her too many questions about Roark in return.

★　★　★

Julia had been on the same tour to Paris a few months ago, but she didn't mind going there again. Once she started her course, she wouldn't be able to afford any kind of holiday. This tour ended on the 22nd of December, and then she intended to travel with Gran to her parents for Christmas.

On the 17th, Julia met the tour members at St Pancras and the journey with the Eurostar and the coach from Paris to Versailles was accomplished with no problem.

That night the guests attended a concert and spent the night in a nearby luxury hotel.

The following day, they made a guided tour of the Château de Versailles, and after a late lunch, the coach took them to Paris, for the first of four nights. The late afternoon and evening was free. Julia went to explore some of the small streets in Montmartre. It was cold, but the decorations, lights and the cheerful sound of 'Joyeux Noel!' everywhere helped to put her in the right mood for Christmas, even though she thought constantly about Roark and felt the loss even more intensely when she saw two people in love, oblivious to the world around them.

Next day there was a lecture and guided tour around some of the most famous Paris attractions and an afternoon excursion to the Cité de la Musique followed by a magical evening at the Opera to see Swan Lake.

The next morning was free. Julia visited the Galeries Lafayette; lit up like a fairytale castle. The crowds jostled and hurried, everyone carrying packages and Christmas shopping. Julia just enjoyed the atmosphere.

After a coffee in a bistro, she checked the time and decided to return to the hotel. The Metro was full and she was glad to walk the short distance from the station to the hotel in the fresh air.

She entered the foyer and looked around. Her heart stood still when she spotted Roark sitting nearby. She had a moment to throttle the dizzying effect he was having on her and to study him before he noticed her. She had her emotions under control when he got up and came towards her.

'Roark! What are you doing here?'

'I came looking for you.'

'Me, why? Something wrong with Gran?'

He took her upper arm and shook his head. 'No. Let's go into the bar, it's quieter in there.'

Trying to hide her intense pleasure, she went wordlessly. Tugging at her scarf, she dispensed with it and struggled with her coat. Her breath was uneven; his nearness was overwhelming.

His eyes were intense. 'I wanted to give you time to adjust after the episode with your gran, but now I decided it was time to sort things out.'

'Sort things out? What exactly?' She hardly dared to ask.

'I wanted to know if you think you can put up with me for longer than a few hours at a time. I won't be surprised if you tell me to go to hell — but I hope you won't.'

She was perplexed but managed to reply. 'Of course I can put up with you; for much longer than a couple of hours. I'm sorry I was so mean to you that morning you dropped me off at the hospital. I didn't mean to be so hurtful. I thought about getting in touch to tell you so, but didn't quite have enough courage.'

'I understand. It was thoughtless of me to comment on your private life when you were so worried about your gran. I chose the wrong subject but I didn't mind what you said — you were right, I was blind to Kiara's behaviour for too long. In comparison, you've always been honest and I think you understand me. We're on the same wavelength most of the time.'

'Are we?'

'Most people tend to pander to me. I don't know if it's because I'm a professor, or for some other reason. You've never done that. You've always treated me like a friend. In the beginning, I didn't know how to handle that. It took a time until I began to appreciate your honesty and the way you still managed to respect my feelings. You showed a lot of understanding.'

Her heart thumped uncomfortably. 'Oh, don't exaggerate Roark. You know dozens and dozens of people. You were married. Of course you know lots of people who understand you.'

He shook his head slowly. 'Not in the way you do. I've never had this kind of connection with anyone else before. You know how I'll react almost before I do.'

She swallowed and waited.

'At the time, I didn't want to get involved with anyone again. I blocked you out, I pushed you away, and it was only later that I realised I'd robbed myself of the chance of something terribly important.'

She laughed shakily. 'If this is an apology, don't go any further. Our conversations and bickering were never a one-way street. If you think it's necessary for you to explain, please don't. If we can be friends, I'm genuinely glad. I wouldn't want us to be adversaries.'

'And we can't be more than friends?'

She shifted and clutched her hands tighter, her mind racing. 'Roark, you made it perfectly clear that you didn't want to let any other woman into your life again. I hope you'll be happy whatever you decide to do. Claudia told me that your ex-wife was back in London, so I wondered if you'd decided to give your marriage a second chance — not that it's any of my business.'

He ran his hand through his hair. 'I was stupid when I told you about not wanting to ever take a chance again. I believed it at the time.' He paused and looked puzzled. 'What did you say about my ex-wife?'

Julia looked down at the uninteresting grey carpet. 'When we met at the office recently, you were with your sister and another woman.'

'And?'

'I wondered if she was your wife. I wondered if you were trying to re-establish your marriage.'

He looked extremely surprised. 'Fiona? She's Keith's wife, not mine.' He ran his fingers through his hair. 'Yes, my wife is back. How does Claudia know that she's in London? Perhaps Kiara's run out of money and hoping to squeeze some more out of me, but she'll be disappointed.'

Waves of relief swept over her. Julia shrugged. 'After we'd squabbled outside the hospital, I didn't think I'd ever see you again. I told myself it was none of my business.'

'And now that you know the truth and how things stand? I know you're free at the moment, your gran told me, and you know that I'm free, I'm telling you that now.'

'What do you expect me to say?' She licked her lips. 'Do you want me to say I hope you'll find someone to make you happy one day? I do, and I think you deserve someone better than your ex-wife. I think you're capable of love and devotion again if you meet the right person. Deep down we all want that, don't we.'

'Do you?'

'Yes.'

'Will you give me a chance to find out if your hopes and mine are the same? Will you give us the chance to get to know one another properly and fall in love?'

She caught her breath and gloried briefly in the moment. 'Do you think that it's possible?'

'Yes, I do. I've never wanted to be with someone as much as I do with you. You're my other half.'

She nodded; her eyes were shining and a warm glow was beginning to spread throughout her being. 'I know what you mean.'

Taking her into his arms, she felt her knees weaken as his mouth descended. Raising his face, he gazed into her eyes, then he recaptured her lips and his kiss became more demanding and tantalizing. Her thoughts spun and her emotions whirled and skidded. She was certain he was all she ever wanted. How could any woman have thrown someone like him aside?

He let out an audible breath and asked, 'Was that a 'proper' kiss?'

Laughter bubbled up. 'Not bad. With some practise we'll be perfect eventually,' she replied with a mischevious twinkle in her eye.

With a look of complete delight, he kissed the tip of her nose, then her eyes, and finally, he satisfyingly kissed her soft lips.

She had a burning desire for him and ached for another kiss.

'What's on your agenda for this evening? Is there any chance of chucking your responsibilities so that we can go out and celebrate?'

'We're visiting the Opera at the Bastille, a performance of something by Richard Strauss. Perhaps the lecturer will oblige, but I can't force her to.'

'Leave that up to me! If I use the name Ellis often enough, she may be in awe and give in without a fight.' He grinned and Julia's heart lifted. 'We simply have to be together without any interruptions this evening — if she doesn't agree you'll just quit your job on the spot. This is the start of a special journey, our journey together into the future.'

'Roark . . . I don't intend changing my plans to take that teaching course. You realise that, don't you? I intend to finish my training and become a teacher. And I also never, ever want to be compared to your ex-wife in any way; now or at any time in the future.'

He threw back his head and laughed loudly. 'I should hope not. You are quite, quite, unique. I'd just like to be there with you and support you when you reach your goal, and I'm sure our future depends on us being together and respecting what the other wants. I've learned that I ought to grab happiness with both hands, and I'm trying to grab you with all my might. I think that my happiness depends on you, and I only hope you think the same about me. Together we are strong, and nothing will ever come between us — even if we do squabble now and then!'

She nodded and realised they had both come out of the shadows of the past and had found something wonderful, unwavering, that would carry them into the future — their shared future.

He kissed her once more, pulling her close. 'Let's go and find the lecturer. What's her name? If someone in Paris doesn't understand that two people in love want to be on their own for a while, then this world is lost.'

After he'd helped her into her coat, she slid her hand round his waist and rested her head against him. 'We won't take no for an answer, will we?'

THE END

We do hope that you have enjoyed reading this large print book.

Did you know that all of our titles are available for purchase?

We publish a wide range of high quality large print books including:
Romances, Mysteries, Classics
General Fiction
Non Fiction and Westerns

Special interest titles available in large print are:
The Little Oxford Dictionary
Music Book, Song Book
Hymn Book, Service Book

Also available from us courtesy of Oxford University Press:
Young Readers' Dictionary
(large print edition)
Young Readers' Thesaurus
(large print edition)

For further information or a free brochure, please contact us at:
Ulverscroft Large Print Books Ltd.,
The Green, Bradgate Road, Anstey,
Leicester, LE7 7FU, England.
Tel: (00 44) **0116 236 4325**
Fax: (00 44) **0116 234 0205**

Other titles in the
Linford Romance Library:

DESTINY CALLING

Chrissie Loveday

It is 1952. William Cobridge has returned from a trip to America a different man. Used to a life of luxury, he had been sent away to learn about life in the real world. He meets teacher Paula Frost on a visit to see her aunt, the housekeeper at Cobridge House. He is keen to see Paula again and asks her for a date. Could this be the start of a new romance? But then, things never go smoothly . . .

WHERE I BELONG

Helen Taylor

When a mysterious Italian man arrives on the doorstep in a storm, Maria can hardly turn him away, even though the guesthouse is closed for the winter. Maria's gentle care helps Dino recover from his distressing news, and soon she risks losing her heart to this charismatic stranger. But he has commitments that will take him far away, and her future is at the guesthouse. Can two people from different walks of life find a way to be together?

WED FOR A WAGER

Fenella Miller

Grace Hadley must enter into a marriage of convenience with handsome young Rupert Shalford, otherwise Sir John, her step-father, will sell her to the highest bidder. But Rupert's older brother Lord Ralph Shalford has other ideas and is determined he will have the union dissolved. However, Sir John is equally determined to recover his now missing step-daughter. Will Grace ever find the happiness she deserves?

OUR DAY WILL COME

Sally Quilford

When handsome American airman Ben Greenwood walks into the Quiet Woman pub, the landlord's pretty daughter Betty Yeardley is immediately attracted to him. But Betty is promised to Eddie Simpson, who has been missing in action for two years. With a stocking thief putting the villagers of Midchester on edge, and Eddie's parents putting pressure on Betty to keep her promise, she is forced to fight her growing feelings for Ben.